A Score To Settle

by

Joan Emery

Dales Large Print Books
Long Preston, North Yorkshire,
BD23 4ND, England.

British Library Cataloguing in Publication Data.

Emery, Joan
    A score to settle.

A catalogue record of this book is ᴸᴾ
available from the British Library

ISBN   978-1-84262-573-6 pbk

First published in Great Britain in 1995 by D C Thomson

Copyright © 1995 by Joan Emery

Cover illustration by arrangement with
P.W.A. International Ltd.

The moral right of the author has been asserted

Published in Large Print 2007 by arrangement with
Joan Emery

Dales Large Print is an imprint of Library Magna Books Ltd.

Printed and bound in Great Britain by
T.J. (International) Ltd., Cornwall, PL28 8RW

CHAPTER ONE

After her first shocked gasp, Samantha snapped, 'Take your hands off me,' and struggled forward to pull away from the seeking mouth and fleshy fingers of her despised employer.

This time, however, she knew exactly what to do. She bent back one fat finger on each hand and ground her high heel into his foot.

He yelped with pain and she moved behind the desk.

'Believe this, Parker – I am leaving and you will not stop me.'

Glacial calm hid her intense shock at seeing him here. He should have been miles away; she'd made the appointment herself. Thank goodness she had organised her 'leaving present' earlier.

She could hardly bear the sight of him, but

no way would she take her eyes off him. His nauseous smile was in place. He was back to being the jovial, senior partner the rest of the world saw. His knowing nod further incensed her.

'I see you recall my premise, dear Samantha. My word against yours! Not to mention what the local rag would make of your sordid personal life. A word in the right–'

'Just you stop right there,' she spat out, disgust dripping from every word.

Red stained the bull neck and rushed up to colour his flabby cheeks, but before he could move or say another word she continued, 'Listen to this before you try threatening me again, Mr Justice of the Peace Parker... And in case you're wondering – it's not the only copy.'

She switched on the office Dictaphone and heard her voice telling Parker she would take him to the Tribunal if he didn't stop trying to force his sexual attentions on her.

Then his voice came clearly, 'Now, my

dear, you know you won't do that. Even though we know what you say is true, who would believe you against a law-abiding JP like me?'

Parker, white-faced, sat on the nearest chair, his mouth gaping fish-like as he watched Sam's hand deny him speech, had he been capable.

'There's another little nugget you should hear.'

And they both heard the chuckle of the silent listener, then, 'Come now, sweetheart, you know I want you. We'll have such wicked pleasure, you and I. I'll–'

Samantha pressed the switch, she could not bear to hear more, even though she knew she was free.

'Sounds like a bit from a sleazy, third rate film, doesn't it?'

She pointed a finger at the little machine. 'That is your copy. My copy is in my solicitor's safe. Signed, sealed and delivered.'

She turned a cold smile on the visibly shrunken old lecher. But even as she smiled, his choleric colour rose again and he ground out, 'Keep looking over your shoulder, because I'll get you for this. You'll pay, never doubt it.'

Sam suppressed a shudder. He knew he could do nothing. She had him.

'Goodbye,' she said triumphantly.

She gathered her coat and bag and strolled from the room, her head high. She had won! She felt ten feet tall. She was an Amazon.

Outside on the pavement a broad grin spread over her face – there were probably not too many five-feet-four-inch Amazons!

By the time she opened the door of her one-bedroom flat, Sam's legs were shaking.

Her mother's prescription for a bad situation had always been a cup of tea. Well, she decided, this was definitely a bad situation, and began to head for the kitchen.

Suddenly, she was too exhausted to bother and, kicking off her shoes, went into the bedroom. The bed was the only reasonably comfortable piece of furniture in the flat.

Though she was so tired just now that she would probably have slept on the proverbial clothes line her brothers always said she could sleep on.

If only Kev and Robert were not so far away. Even Mum and Dad were out in Australia visiting the pair of them. Tears were lurking behind her eyelids as she lay with her eyes closed, but she was too tired to care. And anyway, she wouldn't have told them if they had been here.

The room was dark when Sam woke up and her exhaustion gone. She switched on the bedside lamp and swung her legs off the bed, giving thanks to the previous owners for leaving fitted carpets behind. She hadn't noticed the worn patches after the first week, and though her present life-style was fairly basic compared to her parents' luxurious home, she had not once regretted moving.

Going into the kitchen/living-room she picked up the phone and punched out Faye's number. A breathless Faye answered.

'Hi, Faye. It worked!'

'But I thought he was out today?'

'He was supposed to be, but the pig came in.' It was good to have a friend who didn't need explanations. 'The old finger bending and heel grinding worked wonders.'

'Great! But how do you feel, Sammy?'

'Shaken, not stirred.' Then she shuddered as she recalled Parker's threats. 'Oh, Faye, what am I to do? I walked out today.'

'Good. The foul swine. You couldn't have stayed there, Sam. You could never have put up with that—'

'Yes, but I don't know what I'm going to do about a job. It's not exactly an employee's market out there. Though I think Parker finally got the message when I replayed the tape. And that's a relief. But he is so vicious and vindictive that... If I could afford it, I'd leave Bristol—'

'Good idea. It would be just the thing—'

'But I can't afford to,' she interrupted.

'Let me finish,' her friend demanded. 'Pete says his brother is having trouble with his secretary. Remember, I told you about Mike? He's not a writer, but he's doing this book...'

'Yes, I remember. He's gone to his holiday place in the wilds of Wales or somewhere.'

'Off Wales – it's an island – a bit bleak at this time of year I should think, but at least old Parker wouldn't find you there. What do you think?'

Sam took a deep breath – if only. 'I think it sounds marvellous, Faye.'

'Look, Sammy,' only her brothers had ever called her that until she'd met Faye again. 'Pete will be home soon. He'll know more about Mike. We'll pop round after we've eaten.'

When they did arrive, to her shame, Sam felt tears glaze her eyes. Faye hugged her and refused to listen when Sam castigated herself for being a fool.

'You've every right to be upset,' Faye told her.

'I'm an idiot. But it's been wearing me down – and today...' She shuddered, remembering the revulsion she had felt.

'Good job we brought the brandy,' Pete said cheerfully, going across to the kitchen cupboards and searching for glasses. Small tumblers had to do. He poured a token thimbleful for his pregnant wife and a generous measure for Sam and himself. He gave the girls theirs then fetched a chair from under the kitchen table and joined them.

'So, how do you feel about working on a small, windswept, rain-soaked island for a month?' he asked.

Sam grinned at the 'enticing' picture. 'Sounds perfect to me.'

'It's not as bad as it sounds,' Faye said encouragingly. 'Mike has a generator, bottled gas and even a mobile phone, so it's not exactly camping. I thought he might need someone, didn't I?' she asked, turning to her husband.

'Poor old Mike hired a male secretary because he thought a guy would be less trouble,' Pete explained. 'But now it seems poor George can't stand Mike's messy ways – or some such excuse – and wants off the island.'

'Oh, dear,' was totally inadequate by way of a remark, but Sam couldn't think what else to say.

'Exactly,' Pete said very seriously. 'I'm to make sure the next secretary is not too fastidiously fussy about a few crumpled cushions. Er, you aren't too fussy, are you?'

He ducked as Sam threw a cushion at him.

But her eyes were shining and she said, 'When do I start?'

'I'd no idea it could rain so hard,' Sam shouted at the boatman.

Trying to hold a conversation, even at close quarters, was near impossible with the wind gusting, she was sure, beyond gale force, and smashing the rain so hard against the glass that Sam feared for its safety.

She was just wondering how much more of this she had to take, when the boatman called to her to get ready. Sam looked through the rain-streaked glass and saw they were very close to land.

'I shan't be stoppin' above a minute,' he warned. 'I'm needed at home, what with the missus and kids down with this sickness bug, an' all. I wouldn't ha' come, 'cept Mr Manley sounded so urgent.'

Sam pulled her hood over her head and zipped her waterproof up to her eyes against the onslaught when she stepped outside. At least she didn't have to make the return journey today and that had to be a plus.

There was a slight bump as the engine idled and the boatman manhandled her big, canvas holdalls outside, demanding, 'Look slippy, miss.'

He went past her, throwing one of the bags over to land on the wooden pier and picking up a rope and tossing it all at the same time. A tall figure encased, even more than she was, in wet-weather gear caught the rope and pulled it round a bollard. Another figure similarly dressed caught a

16

second rope from the other end of the boat, fastened it, then jumped on board.

'Jump, dammit,' the boatman commanded.

Her other long bag was thrown down and she jumped after it wondering where chivalry had gone.

The tall figure on the little pier cast off first one rope, then the second and in no time the boat was lost beyond the break-water as the rain continued sheeting down.

Mike Manley, as she supposed the man to be, was obviously not given to making unnecessary conversation, or even necessary conversation come to that. Though to be fair, it was hardly the weather to stand about chatting. He came over and Sam looked up, then was alarmed when she saw his eyes, like hers, the only visible part of his face, widen then narrow as he gave a curt nod, turned abruptly and picked up the smaller of her bags, leaving the most cumbersome for her to manhandle – not an easy task in this gear and this weather.

It seemed to her that the male population

delighted in scorning feminism, but they soon jumped on the bandwagon when a woman might need a helping hand.

Faye and Pete had said she would be OK with Mike – but from what she had seen of him so far, she began to doubt it! Struggling against the wind now she was away from the sheltering wall and the rain renewed its vigour, she wondered what she had let herself in for.

CHAPTER TWO

Thoroughly fed up as rain sluiced down, finding a thousand ways inside her ill-named waterproofs to run cold down the back of her neck, Sam decided visiting a small island off the Welsh coast in mid-February was not something she would recommend. And certainly not lugging a large, elongated roll bag and not being able to see where you're going.

'Ooff!' she grunted as she ran into a hard, canvas wall.

Mike Manley had stopped and she'd walked into his back. His knees buckled somewhat when her unwieldy bag smashed into them, but he had the door open already and managed to keep his feet as he stumbled over the step.

She followed and thankfully dropped the

bag. Closing the door after her, she un-zipped the wet gear as fast as she could.

She lifted the handbag strap from her shoulder and over her head, glad to shift the heavy bulk. What with that and her well-endowed bust – the bane of her life – she had looked like a barrel under her water-proof.

An odd sound made her look up and she saw Faye's husband.

'Pete?' For a second she stared, then flung herself at him, relief bursting out all over her.

'Pete, you idiot, what do you think you're playing at?' She was clasped to his chest and her mouth taken by surprise by his.

She pushed away as commonsense asserted itself. Of course, it was relief, she hadn't realised how nervous the big surly figure had made her.

'Where's Faye? What kind of idiot trick is this?'

'Pete didn't tell you we are identical twins?'

Wide-eyed, she shook her head. 'You're Mike?'

He nodded. 'Mike Manley.' Then he grinned and looked so like Pete that Sam smiled back. 'And you are?'

'Samantha Turner – Sam to my friends.'

They shook hands formally but her new boss had already withdrawn into himself.

'Sam!' A resigned look of understanding came over his face. 'Pete didn't tell me you were a woman.'

'Oh! He just told me you needed a secretary – because you'd had trouble with the last one.' She paused. 'And he knew you would be able to trust me.' Her sharp glance spoke loudly. 'He also said I could trust you.'

She shivered, despite the warmth in the cottage. 'If you'd tell me which room is mine, I'll get out of these wet things. Goodness, what weather...'

Bending to pick up her bags, Sam was surprised to see them both lifted out of her way.

'Through here. The stairs are in the kitchen.' Mike went before her, then stood back to let her go up the stairs first.

'I'll follow you,' she said. He shrugged and went up.

He stopped at the first door, indicating, 'This is the bathroom – we have to share.' Then he added, 'Just don't touch my things.'

Startled by the vehemence, she lashed back, 'Why on earth should I want to touch your things?'

He ignored her and went on to the next door. Pushing it open with one bag, he went in dumping both on the bed.

Sam followed close behind him and picked up the bags to put them on the floor. 'They're soaking.'

Shrugging his shoulders, he said, 'I'll make a cup of tea – I expect you could do with something. Dinner'll be another couple of hours yet.'

She almost expected him to duck his head when he went out the door, but reasoned that, though the ceilings were quite low, the door frame was a good height.

The room was not huge, but held the double bed, dressing table and fitted wardrobe comfortably. Wildflower printed curtains and duvet cover were complemented by the soft-green, fitted carpet and there was a small, velvet-covered chair in the same soft-green. Faye was right, this was hardly camping.

She shivered again and unzipped the bag with her thick sweaters in.

'Oh, no!' she groaned.

The rain had seeped inside and, if not soaked, then dampened every single sweater, tracksuit and pair of jeans she owned. She opened the other bag, to find that it was even worse, everything was soaking wet.

Thinking that she could perhaps spread some of the clothes on the towel rail in the bathroom, she gathered up a bundle and headed for the bathroom. She got no farther than the doorway.

Good heavens! Everything – toothbrush,

tube of toothpaste, shaving foam, razor and other ablution paraphernalia – was set out with surgical precision. No wonder he didn't want her to touch his things. She would have a job to maintain such neatness; in fact, the sight of such orderliness made her fingers itch to shuffle through it all.

Did Faye and Pete know he was a tidiness freak? Backing out she returned to her own room and dumped the things on the floor, then went downstairs.

The warmth from the kitchen flushed her cheeks.

'Good timing. Kettle's nearly boiling,' Mike said and she was relieved to hear him sound as friendly as his brother. 'Feel better for dry things?'

'I don't have any dry things. My bags are evidently not waterproof,' she added when she saw his surprise. 'Everything is soaked, or at least very damp. I wondered if you had somewhere where I could dry them.' She made it a question, but was sure this precise man would not care to see clothes strewn about for whatever reason.

'Your personal things could go on the towel rail in the bathroom, then bring the thick stuff down to the living-room. The fire should soon dry anything.' He moved the kettle away from the heat and walked across to the stairs. 'Come on, you'd better have something of mine for now.'

Five minutes later Sam could hardly believe he was the same severe man whose regimented bathroom she had been warned off.

He'd grinned as he'd given her a tracksuit and said, 'These could be a bit on the big side for you.' Then he'd taken the pile of thick clothing downstairs.

Keeping her bra and pants on, but stripping the rest of her clothes, Sam pulled the warm, dry tracksuit top over her head. Snuggling into it, it felt good, she was already warmer. The bottoms were a joke and she couldn't help chuckling as she pulled them up to her armpits. She turned the soft navy cuffs back to find her fingers, then the baggy trousers up several inches to avoid tripping down the stairs.

'Through here!' Mike called, and following his voice she went into a large, but cosy room with a blazing, log fire. She had to admit that it would have looked a typical olde-worlde chintzy, but elegant, sitting-room if all her clothes were not strewn on a variety of vantage points, already steaming gently.

'We can keep them turned to save scorching.' He indicated the jeans in the hearth. 'I keep this fire in all the time. It gives us all our heating and hot water.'

'How on earth do you get fuel?'

'Nature.' He smiled slightly. 'I collect drift wood and anything else likely to burn. There's only us. None of the other cottage owners comes at this time, so there's no competition for fuel.'

I'm not surprised, she said silently. The other owners clearly have more sense!

'Thank you,' she said taking the pretty china mug from him and admiring the flowered design.

'Faye chose the furnishings and such like. She insisted it needed flowers inside because it can sometimes be a bit bleak outside.'

'She was right. I've never been out in weather like today's. Is it often like that?'

'I don't really know. I'm not usually here at this time of year.'

He cut two hefty chunks of fruit cake and, handing her one piece on a plate, settled himself on the floor with the other. His long legs were drawn up and he leaned back against the heavy, soft-stuffed sofa while he ate thoughtfully and watched the flames.

Suddenly curious about cooking and such now she was here in the cottage, it occurred to her she was a bit late.

'About the cooking–' she said. 'I presume we take it in turns?'

'Good Lord, no!'

Sam's temper shot more heat to her face than the log fire, but before she could speak he said, 'You are here only for secretarial work. I'll see to the cooking, and washing up. It we keep the bathroom clean when we use it and our own rooms, there shouldn't be anything to bother about.'

Well, well, she thought, a new man indeed, though that bathroom could pose problems if she allowed her fingers to run amok!

In truth, if Pete had said she would be doing the cooking as well as the typing, she would still have come. She had been so glad to escape Parker, she had not given much thought to the work or the situation on this bleak, world's end island. Not that she'd seen much of it yet. And Wales might be only a mile away as the fish swims, but the unfriendly sea between here and it made civilisation as distant as the moon.

It was very pleasant sitting in the quiet room listening to the logs crackle.

'These walls must be thick, you can't hear the wind in here.'

'It's dropped a bit, but, yes, the walls are thick. And the windows have Scandinavian triple glazing.'

'That sounds horribly expensive for just a

holiday home.'

His look said it was nothing to do with her, but he added, 'Possibly, but at least I know the place is weatherproof and secure.'

Replacing his mug and plate on the tray, he leaned forward and turned her jeans over in the hearth.

'Thanks,' she murmured, 'I can do that.'

'No problem.' And he sat back and watched her shift her other things about.

He'd probably only done it to remind her to remove the mess as soon as possible, she decided.

'There are some books behind there,' he informed her, pointing to the loaded clothes horse beyond the sofa. 'Help yourself. I'll get cracking with dinner, though there's not too much to do – George insisted on preparing the goulash while he waited for the boat.'

Sam knew she should not be surprised at the man's domesticity. Derek, her ex-boyfriend, had always been more than capable in the kitchen.

Checking the clothes and turning them occupied her for some time, and in between times she looked through the shelves of paperbacks. She earmarked quite a few she wanted to read, though she was not in the mood to do so at present.

It was a pleasant meal and they talked, if not like old friends, then interested strangers. Sam was quite impressed with his and George's culinary skills, but did not say so – he might think she was patronising him – Derek would have thought so!

Politeness demanded something, however, and she lifted her wine glass and said, 'My compliments to the chef.'

It was uncanny. He looked so much like Pete when he grinned, otherwise she never thought of his twin.

'Yes?'

Startled, Sam realised she had been staring.

'I'm sorry. I was just thinking it was funny that Faye never said about you and Pete being twins.'

'Ah, that's a family thing. It began with our grandmother, who was also a twin. She and her sister hated being called "the twins" because no-one could tell them apart. Our own mother heard the story so often that she made sure everyone knew which of us was which. Pete and I just carried on the same.'

Sam nodded her understanding.

'Have you known Faye long?'

'Twenty years.' Sam smiled at his surprise. 'Actually, we met again a few months ago at an aerobics class. When we got talking we discovered we had been friends when we first began school at five. Faye's parents moved to the Midlands, but we'd both never forgotten our first schoolfriend. Incredible coincidence, isn't it?'

It may have been the effects of the wine and good food, but Sam was glad she was not expected to work tonight. With her eyelids drooping she checked her clothes in the sitting-room, then said, 'Good-night,' and went up to bed.

CHAPTER THREE

When Sam went downstairs the next morning, the first thing she noticed was all her clothes neatly folded in two piles on a kitchen chair and the worktop. Mike Manley would be pleased to have his tidy house back to rights!

'Thank you for dealing with my things.' She pointed to the dry clothes. 'I'm sorry to be such a nuisance.'

'I shall expect due payment,' he said pleasantly, but a shaft of fear struck sharp inside Sam's head and she felt herself lose colour.

He looked askance. 'Good grief, woman. What do you think I mean? I only meant so you would work hard at the typing for me – nothing else. Is that understood?'

'Perfectly, thank you.'

She took a mug of tea he handed her and decided not to try and excuse her singular lack of trust. There was no way Faye and Pete would have let her come here if there was any doubt about his integrity. And she certainly was not about to explain Parker's offers of salary increases and week-end business trips where he would 'expect due payment.' It was all she could do not to shudder as she remembered Parker's lustful leer.

'Perhaps I should make it clear that I am interested only in getting this book finished.' He paused, then added, 'I won't lie to you. I find your face and figure very attractive, not to say tempting, given different circum-stances.'

Was she supposed to be grateful for that? He shrugged his shoulders and Sam pre-sumed he meant that he may have acted differently if they were not alone on the island and she a friend of his family. Were all men the same? Did he think he was so wonderful, that she would not be able to stop herself falling for him?

She could feel the blood surging up into her cheeks.

'I'm sure that doesn't require comment, Mr Manley.' She had the satisfaction of seeing her dry tone hit the target.

Then he straightened and said, 'It's about time you called me Mike, Sam, if we're to work together.'

It wasn't open to question or choice, so she nodded.

'I'll show you the office, but you might like to know a bit about the story, first.'

She agreed, but he seemed to need to collect his thoughts before he began.

'It's about Jenny, a young girl, very beautiful, who should have avoided men like the plague, but didn't. It's the story of her search for love, her failure to find the kind of love she craved and her journey on the way. It also tells how she should have been looked after and been protected, but was let down, even at the end – another failure.' He looked up. 'And so she died.'

His mouth was pinched and, if the pain in his eyes meant anything, this story was important to him.

When she had the computer switched on Mike indicated the wire stationery tray and went out. She saw the printed title page of 'Jenny's Story' sitting tidily on top of a few sheets of A4 which were on an untidy folder stuffed with handwritten sheets. Sam decided to take a look just to get some idea of the storyline.

She did not want to stop after the first page and the narrator's anger became hers as she read how badly the innocent, eight-year-old Jenny was treated by her mother's lover.

Mike's writing was almost childlike in its simplicity, so it sounded like Jenny writing it. The emotions stirred by the naïve narrative were all the more intense for this. Sam read on and had finished a chapter before she realised it.

She wanted to find Mike Manley right away and tell him what she thought of

'Jenny's Story,' but she quelled the excitement and began typing. She waited until they had eaten lunch then told him and eagerly watched for his reaction.

His closed expression was not what she expected. 'Thank you, Samantha.'

'The beginning is gripping and I can't wait to read the rest,' she persisted.

'Unfortunately, I haven't got the end right yet, and the publisher is pressing for it,' he said, but Sam felt an unaccountable lightening of her spirit as she went back to her typing.

Jenny's story followed the nervous child being taken into care. She was placed with houseparents who were an experienced and very kind couple. From them the little girl learned what being loved by parents really meant. And Sam was relieved to see how two brothers, young teenagers, took her under their wing. Jenny had a fairly normal and happy life with the big family of 'brothers and sisters,' but she always went to Tony with her troubles and to be reassured.

When Mike called Sam for dinner, she wasn't sure what made her think it, but it struck her that there was a strong similarity between Tony in the story and Mike Manley.

Tony might be fair headed and not a twin, but he was a naturally caring lad who looked out for his brother and Jenny. The way Tony's caring was played down, but very apparent to the reader, helped convince her. She had assumed Mike was involved in some way when Pete had first mentioned the book, telling her that he thought his brother was doing the right thing, putting it before the public.

Now, remembering how Mike had spread her damp clothes about to make sure they dried, she was sure he was Tony.

This new idea that Mike was closely involved with Jenny bubbled away inside her. She wanted to blurt it out and ask questions, but his withdrawn expression across the table did not encourage conversation and certainly not quizzing into anything remotely personal. But it was going to be a long old month if she allowed herself to be intimidated into silence too much of the time.

'This is good,' she said, indicating the chilli. He merely tipped his head in acknowledgement.

Well, that didn't work! No conversation there!

'Are Tony and Tim you and Pete?'

Shock tactics. She hadn't really meant to ask like that, but it was probably the best way to get an answer.

She was wrong.

'I don't think it is necessary for you to know the people involved with Jenny.'

He got up from the table.

'OK,' she acknowledged cheerfully, it was not her nature to surrender without a fight of some sort. Then, still determined to have some conversation, she said, 'Did you say there was someone interested in publishing it?'

His frown did not clear entirely, but she must have hit on a safe topic.

'Yes. As a matter of fact a friend of mine is in the publishing business and she is sure the subject will sell well. Not that that is the object of writing the book–'

'You must be the only writer who thinks so.'

'But the more people who read it means, hopefully, more people will understand and the fewer Jennys there will be in the future,' he said as though she had not interrupted. 'Barbara read the first longhand draft. Barbara was terrific. She gave me so much advice and encouragement,' he enthused. 'She even suggested I cut myself off from it personally and rewrite it in story form. She's going to present it to her colleagues once it's in manuscript form. That is where you come in.'

She read that to mean – and that is all you need to know!

'OK,' she repeated casually, 'But I might not be very good at remembering not to question things. You'll just have to tell me to mind my own business.'

She thought she caught a brief flash of a Pete grin, but, no, it was a deeper frown. No-one could accuse Mike Manley of being easy to read!

The following afternoon, Mike said, 'I think you should have a break from that machine. We'll go out for a walk, while it's fine.'

Sam bridled at his manner. So she wasn't to be given a choice in the matter, was she?

'I'll enjoy that. I had wondered if the rain ever stopped.' She found she meant it, and was grateful her commonsense had got in first.

A brief nod acknowledged he'd heard it, but he was clearly not disposed to talk.

Sam was glad she'd wrapped up well against the fierce wind, as the sun tried and failed to break through the clouds. Mike set a formidable pace and she found she was almost running to keep up.

'Hey,' she gasped, catching at his sleeve with her fur-mittened hand, 'if you keep this up – you can go on your own.'

They had both stopped, but he was breathing quite normally she saw.

'I'm sorry, Samantha, I was miles away.'

'Is it the book? Would it help to talk about your problem?'

'No. It wouldn't help.'

They walked on at Sam's pace and he pointed out a few other cottages in the distance with the sea beyond them. They all appeared closed and shuttered to withstand the winter weather.

'Come on.' He turned off before the cottages and led her down a rough hewn path. 'I never come out without taking home something for the fire.'

Sam thoroughly enjoyed herself, beach-combing along the shore and helping pull huge logs above the high water mark. He said he would take a saw to them later.

'I'm glad you're not tiny. Jenny was tiny. Looked like a puff of wind would blow her away. You're not very big, but you are strong, aren't you?'

Sam wasn't sure she wanted him to think

of her like that, but – ye gods, whatever was the matter with her? She couldn't care less how he thought of her!

Sam's pleasure at being beside the sea had dimmed as they carried two very long, but thinnish logs back to the cottage. Mike was in front with a log under each arm and Sam brought up the rear holding the thin ends in her hands. She missed seeing the small boulder, but her foot caught it and she went flying, dropping the wood as she tried to save herself.

'Are you all right?'

The concern in his voice was all a feminine ego could crave as he dashed back to sit her up carefully, and his gentleness as he checked her legs through her trousers made her feel a fraud.

Back inside the cottage she was already starting to feel stiff and actually welcomed his insistence that she have a hot bath. Her trousers were torn across the knees, so it was no surprise to see blood running down her legs when she took them off.

Mike appeared when she came out of the bathroom in her towelling robe and told her he would see to her knees.

'I can manage, thank you,' she said.

'I'm sure you can, but I want to be sure they're clean. We're not exactly handy for the hospital if anything should go wrong.'

On that happy thought, she went into her bedroom and Mike followed.

'Hop up.' He indicated the bed with a curt nod. When she was settled, he lifted the robe to bare her knees.

It was all Sam could do not to snatch at it and cover her knees. What was the matter with her? She gasped when the antiseptic stung the first wound.

'Sorry,' Mike said, glancing up before carrying on. His grim face brought her back to reality and she concentrated on watching his handiwork.

'There, that should keep it clean. I don't suppose you've kept your tetanus shots up to date.'

'As a matter of fact I have. So there! The

hospital insisted when I cut myself on a corned beef tin last year and couldn't stop the bleeding.'

'A common enough accident, and that's one worry less. Though, another time, I'll make sure my secretary is not accident prone before leaving civilisation.'

'Oh, are you thinking of making this a regular winter pastime?' she asked sweetly.

He picked up the first aid kit and raised his eyebrows at her as he left her room. Looking at the closed door, she stretched a smile. Those sardonic eyebrows reminded her of the hero in one of the romances her brothers used to tease her for reading.

Hmmph! She had never thought of Pete like that, so what made him different from his twin – Faye probably.

It had been Sam's lucky day when Pete Manley needed to expand his Birmingham based computer software business and opened an office and warehouse in Bristol. Faye had come back to Bristol just when Sam needed a good friend. It had helped to talk about Parker and it had been Faye's idea to go to self-defence classes.

Just the thought of Parker made her wonder why she was not permanently off men. The voice of reason told her it was because she was not a fool! Of course, not all men were foul, and having a father and two brothers who were decent men helped to keep her sense of proportion.

However, too many were rotten, if the story she was typing was true, and from the way both Pete and Mike said the story needed telling, and Mike talked about Jenny being tiny, she was sure it was true.

She shrugged. She should be getting on with it, not reclining on her bed. She hadn't hurt herself so badly that she needed rest. Mike Manley had treated her as though she were fine china, which had been pleasant enough, because it was a new experience, but she had always been tough and resilient, her brothers had made sure of that. She put a loose tracksuit on and went down into the office to get on with her work.

'What do you think you're doing?' Mike said from the doorway. He startled her and Sam stopped typing.

'I should have thought it was obvious,' she snapped and turned back to the keyboard. What was the matter with the man? She was here to work, wasn't she?

'You're all right.' The dull statement must have been for himself; there was no need for her to add more. Not that he waited; he'd gone when she glanced over her shoulder.

Later on it took all of Sam's control not to flinch as Mike came into the room. She blinked to come back to the Welsh cottage – she'd been in a dingy flat in London's East End, feeling every blow that Jenny had taken from the man she loved. When life was not going Jim's way – he hit her; he lost his job, yet again, he hit her. He got drunk at the pub, came home – hit her – then he pleaded for forgiveness. But when she told him she was having a baby, he became furious and beat her so violently she miscarried.

Sam relaxed her hunched shoulders. 'This

is powerful stuff, Mike,' she told him with a little smile, forgetting for the moment that he seemed not to want to talk to her about it.

'Yes,' he said without turning back.

Perhaps he was in the throes, or whatever writers get themselves into, of his last chapters and didn't want the present intruding.

'I take it as a compliment you're so involved you don't hear, Sam.'

For the second time that day she stopped typing and needed a moment or two to be aware of her surroundings.

Glancing up she saw her employer standing in the doorway watching as she stretched and rubbed the back of her neck.

'Dinner.'

'That's good, I'm starving...' Her voice wavered and she stood still when he didn't move from his position.

'So am I,' he said, then turned his back and went into the kitchen.

Sam stayed where she was. Had she imagined that look? In the last few months, since she said goodbye to Derek, her life had turned upside down. What was it about her that seemed to attract male attention wherever she went? It wasn't as though she deliberately went out of her way to be noticed. And now Mike? He had said he found her attractive... Though from the way he had spoken about the girl in the story, sweet, little things in need of protection were his type. She straightened her shoulders and grinned. She might not be very tall, but no-one had ever described Samantha Turner as a sweet, little thing. She followed Mike into the kitchen.

'It smells delicious,' she commented and knew that had it been Pete Manley who had prepared the meal she would have told him he would make someone a lovely wife, but this forbidding-looking man did not encourage her sense of fun.

Determined not to be frozen into silence, Sam said, 'Did you go back for the logs?' She sat up and looked expectant.

A muscle pulled at the corner of his mouth and she wondered if he had read her mind.

'Yes, I did. I told you, I never go out without bringing something back.'

The following day a fresh breeze lifted Sam's hair as she made her way down the steep rocky path to the beach. The spite had gone from the wind and there was no need to huddle tight in her anorak today.

Mike had declined her invitation to come out, but that in itself was something. He must trust her not to have another accident.

She trod carefully over the assorted pebbles, reaching the sandy water's edge as the sun came from behind the clouds. She stood with her eyes closed, feeling the warmth of its rays on her face. It was wonderful. She hadn't realised how much she'd missed the sun.

Keeping her eyes open for flotsam to carry back to the cottage, or tell Mike about, she walked on just out of reach of the small, but energetic, waves. There was a wonderful sense of freedom, a sense of safety.

'A sense of usefulness, even,' she said out loud and laughed at herself as she went to lug a sizeable tree trunk from the water to above the tidemark.

It was a bit much for her, but she was not going to be beaten, and pulled, pushed and rolled the great log to safety. Squatting beside the thing to get her breath, she decided to leave any more that size to chance and Mike Manley.

A fall of stones tumbled down the cliff face about twenty yards away and she glanced up in time to catch sight of the back of Mike's navy-blue anorak.

'Think of the devil and he's sure to appear,' she misquoted to herself. Surely the man could have acknowledged her fine effort, but perhaps she was maligning him, perhaps he was fetching a saw for the log.

She waited out of interest, to see how he dealt with sawing logs on the ground. Her father always used a log horse. Not that her dad had much need of his horse at the moment, unless he was sawing logs for the 'barbies' while he and Mum were in Australia.

Mike Manley was taking his time. It didn't take fifteen minutes to go to the cottage and back! Impatient, Sam walked on. It was a pleasant day, but still too cold to stand about, and she needed the exercise.

Making her usual effort at conversation when they were eating their evening meal, she commented, 'It was quite pleasant out, wasn't it?' Then remembering her fine effort hauling the tree trunk she went straight on, 'Did you find the log? It was a good size wasn't it?'

She stopped to give Mike the chance to say something, but he was looking puzzled.

'Do you mean to say you didn't go back for it?'

'I didn't go out at all this afternoon–'

'I saw you up on the clifftop–'

He was shaking his head very definitely.

'You couldn't have.'

Mike's cold statement shut her up, but she made sure disbelief showed on her face.

'It was probably a bird – the wing span of a cormorant can be quite impressive.'

Sam wondered why he did not want her to know he had been out of the cottage that afternoon.

'It was probably some other fool who's decided February is a good time to visit his holiday home.'

She didn't care if she was being rude, it annoyed her to know he thought her silly enough to mistake a bird for him.

CHAPTER FOUR

Taking stock of things as she climbed down the path to the beach a couple of days later, Sam decided she could get used to having her meals prepared and the washing up done, while all she had to do was type in the morning, go for a walk in the afternoon and work a few hours in the evening after dinner. Quite the little holiday! And if Mike Manley had been more friendly life might have been really enjoyable. Obviously that attraction he had admitted to had worn off pretty rapidly, but then, she was not his type, thank goodness.

Sam kicked a stone into the water. Her companion in residence had gone politely cold on her, but better the frozen-featured gentleman than an amorous boss chasing her round the island. A mental picture of the lecherous Parker was snuffed out almost before she registered it, and she grabbed at a fair-sized log at the water's edge.

Dumping the log out of reach of high tide, she admitted, in her usual honest fashion, that her walks had lost their sparkle and, try as she might, she just did not find the same pleasure mooching along the beach alone.

She had not seen Mike again when she was out, though she had seen the big, black birds and every time she did she got more furious with the stupid man. She could tell the difference between a man and a bird!

She knew Mike's side of the island quite well and decided to have a closer look at the other holiday homes. Whatever other thoughts she had she still enjoyed this freedom to wander at will; this feeling of safety she had knowing there were only the two of them on the island. Never going into deep countryside on the mainland by herself, deeming it not sensible for a woman alone, she found it doubly pleasurable here.

Twigs and small branches, victims of the

gales, littered her path and snapped under-
foot as she walked through the few stunted,
leaf-bare trees. A few primroses had bravely
opened their flowers and bluebells were
pushing their new growth skywards. Sam
could picture the soft, blue carpet in a few
weeks' time.

She walked on, but had looked at only two
other cottages by the time she decided to
wend her way home. She was hungry and
would be glad to get back for her meal.
Then she understood why. There was a
faint, but distinct smell of meat cooking and
her gastric juices were doing their stuff.

She was still some way from the cottage,
but the air must be so clear here that smells
travelled farther.

She knew she had imagined the scent of
roasting meat when she got back to the
cottage. There was only tinned and packet
food, tasty, but nothing like a roast chicken
or rabbit.

'Chicken supreme à la Manley,' Mike said
with a flourish that reminded her of Pete, as

he set their food on the table.

'Looks delicious.' She ate a forkful. 'Tastes delicious,' she told him, nodding approval. 'I was ready for it. It was odd, but I thought I smelled meat barbecuing while I was out.' She laughed. 'I was probably thinking about my family in Australia.'

'I didn't realise you were Australian. You don't have an accent.'

'I'm not,' she said. 'But both of my brothers are married to Australian girls and live out there. My parents are visiting them.' She smiled and told him, 'We joked about all the barbies Mum and Dad would have while they were there.'

'Is there only you left in Bristol, or do you have more brothers and sisters?'

'No, there are only the three of us. I was the baby of the family.'

'Hmm.'

She saw the half smile as though he had just figured something out and it was not anything in her favour, but she was enjoying his mellow mood and let it pass.

'Did you enjoy your walk? I saw you come back from the other direction.'

'It was quite pleasant. Have you been here when the bluebells are out?'

He nodded. 'May is usually the best time to see them. In fact, in spring it is a nature lover's paradise with the flowers and the seal pups on the rocks, and birds nesting all over the island. You have to be careful if you want to walk anywhere, as they nest among the flowers, among the stones and in every crevice and crack in the cliffs.'

'Then I'm sorry you didn't decide to write up your book in spring,' she told him.

Later, when she was typing the manuscript, Sam reflected that it had been a pleasant meal for a change. Not that he was ever nasty, but talking had been easier tonight.

Next day, she made her way across the island to take a look at more cottages. She enjoyed being nosey, curious to see how the owners had tried to make each cottage their own.

It was quite sheltered in the tiny bay, but Sam was amazed to see one trusting soul had left his dinghy and outboard with only a light tarpaulin for protection.

'Blow his luck,' she said out loud. 'Imagine trying to start that engine after the kind of weather we've just had.'

Walking back she caught a glimpse of Mike's navy anorak as he ducked behind a bush. Stupid man! I suppose he'll tell me it was another bird! What on earth was wrong with him?

If he didn't want to acknowledge her outside, she wasn't going to give him the satisfaction of knowing she had seen him! She deliberately turned her head from his direction and walked on.

What was that? She stopped, alert, ready to run. Something had swished past her head and hit a tree farther on. The thwack it made registered. Now, she did look round, but there was no sign of him.

He had gone too far this time. Whatever he'd thrown had been too close for comfort.

It could have hit her; could have done damage. She would give him a piece of her mind.

She hurried on as her thoughts came thick and fast. She would get back to the cottage first and be waiting for him.

The door was open when she got back. Surely she would have seen him if he had been in front of her? She went inside calling his name. Then went through to the kitchen, but there was no sign of him in there, nor in the office. She went to the bottom of the stairs to listen for sounds from above, nothing. He must be in the living-room; but again there was no sign.

She turned back and nearly jumped out of her skin as he came in through the doorway breathing heavily. His arms were full of logs and he nodded his acknowledgement then waited for her to step aside so he could stack the logs beside the fireplace.

She wanted to mention that whatever he had been chucking about had just missed her, but what was the point? Caustic thoughts spun through her head and she went upstairs to be alone. She needed to think. Something was not right.

'Hi, Pete,' Mike said into his mobile phone, 'problems?'

'Now why would there be anything I can't handle? No, all is well, but I thought I'd give you a call...'

Mike knew his brother and waited to hear what was bothering him.

'It's probably nothing, but Faye heard a warning on the radio for your area. It seems a prisoner has escaped – GBH and all that, and don't approach said prisoner – and now they've discovered a boat is missing. I made a few calls just to check it out and I gather those gales you've had could have blown that boat your way.'

Mike spoke into the short silence.

'Sam said, the other day, she had seen someone. She thought it was me, but I wasn't out at the time.'

'Do you want me to alert the police?'

'Be as well to mention it, but I'll go round the island and check now before the light goes. It could have been a bird she saw.'

'OK, but don't forget the grievous bodily harm stuff, Mike, in case it wasn't. Pity you haven't a weapon of some sort. I'll ring later with any more news this end, but let me know how you get on.'

Mike double locked the door and set off, feeling it was all a bit unlikely, but was glad of the hefty poker held loosely up his sleeve. There was no point telling Sam. She was probably reading while she waited for dinner. If it was the escaped prisoner she had seen, she would be safer inside the cottage and it would be easier to try and find tell-tale traces without worrying about her. He certainly did not anticipate an unnecessary confrontation. He was no hero. The police could come and deal with the fellow, if it was him.

He skirted the stony hillocks, looking for soft ground that might show footprints. He saw a few small ones that must belong to

Sam, then he stopped, staring at a mark across one of Sam's. It was difficult to work out if Sam had stopped, then turned, or if it was part of a larger shoe print. It wasn't his, he had not been this way since last year.

Damn, it was his own fault, he should have listened more carefully to Sam; asked where she thought she'd seen him. It would have given him something to go on. But at the time he had been trying not to act like an idiot – trying to keep his cool when they were together – when he wanted to make her laugh, talk about her, about him, about them…

Pete had asked after Sam only a couple of days ago. He had said she'd had a rough time recently, but he knew Mike would take good care of her. Perhaps Pete had picked up his growing feelings for Sam? He must keep his distance. And just as well, with the weight of guilt about Jenny pressing on him…

The light was almost gone when he spotted the boat below him on one of his cliff-edge sorties. There was no point going down for a closer inspection because he could see it was smashed up and by the time he found a way down this part of the cliff it would be too dark to see.

That was proof enough for tonight and Mike went swiftly back to the cottage.

When he saw the glow of light from Sam's room, he wondered, should he tell her about the escaped prisoner and the smashed boat? No, he would tell her in the morning. She might worry all night for nothing.

But Sam was worrying already, worrying like mad. She'd seen Mike leave the cottage and, determined to see just what he was up to, swiftly slipped her boots and anorak on to follow him, only to be foiled by the double-locked door.

She hunted for another key. Surely she was not meant to be a prisoner? But why would he go out and lock her in? What was he up to?

She tried the windows, but there was no chance of her getting them open without keys. The door at the back of the office was heavily bolted and locked, but there was no key in the lock. She needed a key. After searching every obvious place, she plundered drawers she'd not noticed before – still no key. Surely the kitchen must reveal one door key – she didn't care which door she got out of.

Rising anxiety was stopping her thinking clearly. She must stay calm. But she was a prisoner, her mind screamed.

What dreadful thing was he doing out there that he needed to make sure she didn't witness? And suppose there was a fire? She would be trapped.

Thoughts of every description and colour flooded her mind before she took hold of herself.

She must not panic. She must think this through. Had he meant to keep her in while he went out this time? He must have. All sorts of nasty little ideas entered her head. Mike was suffering from some terrible illness. He was having a breakdown; was not responsible for his actions. Surely Pete would be aware of it when they spoke on the phone? They were twins, weren't they? Shouldn't Pete know how Mike was feeling?

The story from an old black and white movie she'd seen on television recently came to mind. There was one very good twin, but her sister was the negative twin, capable of anything, even murder. What if that was Mike – what then? Commonsense came to her rescue before she went too far down that path. Of course, it was nonsense. It was only a story.

Yet why would Mike lock her in? Had he done it before when she had been working in the office? Or in her bedroom? This time she would ask questions and demand answers! And she would not be put off with stupid excuses.

She felt better now her mind was made up and went through to the lobby to take off her anorak and boots.

The key in the door alerted her to Mike's return and she stood up, backbone stiff, to watch him come in.

Obviously her presence by the door surprised him and he held up the keys, giving
her a sheepish grin.

'Sorry, habit. I'm afraid I locked you in.
I'm usually here on my own,' he explained.
'I hope you didn't try to get out. I've never
shown you where the spares are, have I?'

She was torn – did she believe him? Or
demand explanations? He pulled at the
bottom of the nearest kitchen wall unit and
the side opened to reveal a slim cupboard
with a row of keys, screwdrivers and such.
The tight knot unwound itself in her
stomach, but she still wanted answers. This
last half hour had shaken her too much.

Until now she had hung on to the con-
viction that Faye would never have allowed
her to come here if there'd been anything to
be concerned about.

She watched him pour two glasses of wine,
then accepted one as he said, 'I have an
apology to make, Sam.'

The seriousness of his tone brought her
full attention.

'That man you thought was me, and I said was probably a bird, may well have been an escaped prisoner.' He hurried on despite her gasp of horror. 'Pete phoned earlier. There was a boat missing as well – there's one smashed on the rocks, round the farthest headland. I've been out having a look. I'm sorry I doubted you, Sam.'

She felt quite light with relief, but not for long as she listened with horror to Mike telling Pete what he had seen and how lucky he thought Sam had been walking about the island.

'Oh, Mike,' she said when he came off the phone, 'I felt so safe walking about by myself. It doesn't bear thinking of. But what do we do now?'

'The police say we should stay locked inside the cottage until they contact us. They'll be over at first light.'

'And this place is quite secure,' she said with feeling.

He grinned. 'Yes, it is. One of the boys we grew up with started his own business and I gave him a free hand to make my house and this cottage burglar proof, as well as the factory, and I think he did a good job.'

Sam agreed wryly. 'You can tell him from me, he made a perfect job of it. It was a thoroughly nasty feeling not being able to find any means of escape.'

'I really am sorry. I should have shown you the key cupboard when you first arrived, but I can only suppose I was taken aback with you being a woman...'

They talked over dinner as never before. Mike seemed willing to talk about Jenny and about the book.

'Does it upset you to type the details of Jenny's appallingly miserable life?'

'Yes, it does. It would upset anyone. It makes me want to do something to help her, but, of course, I know it's too late.' She shrugged her shoulders helplessly.

'I know. I often wonder if I'll ever stop feeling responsible. If only I could have done something more to prevent Jenny taking her own life and her baby's.'

'I didn't realise she had committed suicide – poor Jenny. Though perhaps she thought it was her only way out – the only way to escape from Jim?'

'I should have found some way–'

'If a person is determined, there is no way,' she said gently, putting her hand sympathetically over his.

Very early next morning Mike's phone rang again. It was Pete.

'Thought you'd want to know – the police have just been on. The coastguards have found the guy they were looking for, dead, in the sea, down the coast from you. Probably been dead a couple of days. So you can go back to enjoying your winter interlude on sunny Maidens...'

Dear heaven, how could she have thought Mike Manley was a tidiness-freak, Sam wondered. Stepping into the bathroom after him in the morning, it looked as though he'd done battle with his shaving gear and toothbrush.

Every single thing that had been set out in the bathroom so precisely the day she arrived had never once since then been near to being put back in the same place.

Even by her standards, which were not perfect, Mike Manley was a disgrace. The only thing, two things actually, that saved him being a complete slob in the bathroom, he put the top on his toothpaste and he always folded his towel. And she never touched his things. If someone was turning thumbscrews to force her to confess, she might admit to wanting to do a tiny bit of tidying.

'Good news,' Mike greeted her as she came downstairs. 'Well, it is for us. Not so good for the escapee. They've found him, drowned. Pete phoned earlier to tell me the coastguards pulled the body out of the sea, just down the coast from here. So we are no longer under siege.'

Later, Sam wandered along the beach feeling a bit disappointed. Mike had seemed so much more friendly since yesterday afternoon, and she had rather hoped he might suggest coming out with her. He hadn't.

The beach was almost non-existent and Sam concentrated on finding her usual stone to step on to get round the jutting cliff. Then everything happened at once. Stones rained down the cliff-face, making her look upwards. She screamed and fell backwards when her foot slipped as a boulder hurtled down.

A calm part of her brain saw her stepping stone split apart by the boulder, but even as she shielded her head with her arms and scrambled to her feet, she looked up in case more rocks were falling.

You're no bird, Mike Manley! The hooded anorak was already turning away, but he knew she'd seen him this time. Real horror grabbed her throat. That was deliberate! He wanted to harm her.

CHAPTER FIVE

'Sam!' She heard the shout just behind her and swung round, nearly losing her balance again. He was so close. She grabbed up a rock, her heart racing enough to burst, and faced Mike as he scrambled over the rocks to her.

'Don't touch me!' she shrieked, her weapon raised, and ready to fight to the death. She backed away, unsteady on the pebbles, watching the ludicrous expression come and go on the face.

'You can't think that...?' He looked up at the clifftop and stretched his arm towards her, but she stepped out of his reach not taking her eyes off him.

'For goodness' sake, Sam. You can't think – let's get away from here. Just how do you think I could be up there and down here at the same time?'

He was right. It could not have been Mike. There was no way he could have got down to the beach so fast, when she had seen him moments before up there – and Mike wasn't wearing a navy blue anorak.

Mike was on her side. She lowered the stone.

'OK?' he asked gently. The fight had gone out of her and she was glad when he put his arm round her. 'Come on. We'll be better off back inside the cottage.'

'Who was it, if the police say they've found their man?'

'I haven't a clue,' he confessed. 'It's almost too much of a coincidence that there might be two prisoners on the run. And the police would have said.'

Sam could not help looking over her shoulder at the clifftop as they hurried along the firm, wet sand at the water's edge. Neither spoke, and Sam knew Mike was thinking the same as her. The steep path up to the cottage was ripe for another ambush.

'You wait here,' he said. 'I'll go up and check–'

'No!' She told him. 'I'm coming with you. Two pairs of eyes will be better than one.'

'All right, but I'm going first.' All was quiet. Without a word both of them trod carefully, making as little noise as possible, listening, watching...

A stone clattered down among the rocks nearby and Sam's breath froze. Standing rocklike, they scanned every inch of cliff against the skyline. Nothing...

There was a movement farther down. An iron band tightened around her scalp. Then they watched a herring gull stretching its elegant wings before folding them neatly and settling itself. With a little grin Mike reached back, took her hand and gave it a gentle squeeze. A simple gesture was just what she needed and she gladly left her hand in his as they continued up.

Once safely inside the cottage, Mike poured a couple of brandies. He picked up the phone, checking on the kitchen wall for a number, punched it and waited. After a long wait, his call was answered, but from the one-sided conversation Sam gathered that Bill the boatman was not at home.

'It will be quicker to get Pete to organise help,' he said as he punched another number and without preliminaries told his brother, 'Pete, we're in trouble. The guy is still on Maidens and–'

He stopped abruptly, his face quite savage as he listened.

'They can't have,' he said. 'Someone is definitely here on the island – and damned near killed Sam!'

Not able to hear Pete's response, Sam sat down and slowly sipped her brandy.

'Yes, she is all right–' Mike stopped again, then barked, 'It doesn't matter how, dammit – he tried to drop a boulder on her. Fortunately it missed, but it was too flaming close… But Pete, whoever it is, we need to be away as soon as we can. Bill and his wife are on an outing to London today, so he's not there to fetch us.'

Mike listened again to his brother, then said, 'And you organise the police as well – they need to sort this maniac out.'

Sam was glad Mike saw the urgency of leaving Maidens and hoped Pete could arrange something straight away, now, before daylight went.

'Thanks, Pete. Let me know how you get on.'

He put the phone down and turned to Sam.

'Pete says the police had no doubt the body was their escaped prisoner. It had been in the sea several days.'

'Several days? Then it never was him on the island. Whoever it was threw something at me yesterday.'

'Threw something? And you thought it was me?' He looked at her, incredulous. She didn't try to excuse herself. 'Why didn't you say something?'

'I was going to, but I thought you carrying logs in was part of the same elaborate charade. Then, when you locked me in, I was convinced…'

Mike's face creased into an understanding grimace and he came round the table to squeeze Sam's shoulders.

'Poor Sam, you have had a rough time of it since you came here. I know some of it has been my fault, but I'll get you out of this mess as soon as I can. I promise.'

She looked up at him, finally convinced she could trust him. A small, satisfied glow settled inside her, though since hearing Pete's news she had begun having horrible thoughts. Did Mike know about Parker? Had Pete told him about her ex-boss?

'Who do you think it is?' she asked.

He said matter of factly, 'Heaven knows! But start packing. There's nothing we can do now except wait. We'll be safe enough in here.'

Should she tell him what she'd been thinking? It could be a professional job, a man hired specially to frighten her, harm her. Until she'd worked for Parker she hadn't known such vindictive people existed outside films and books.

She would be relieved to get away from Maidens, but where should she go? Parker knew where she lived. She couldn't go back to the flat just yet. When she saw Pete she would ask him to see Parker and tell the vile creature that if he did not leave her alone, she would go to the police. Yes, that was it. Meanwhile she would stay in her parents' home. She would feel safe there. Parker knew nothing about her family.

Unless it became absolutely necessary, she did not want to explain to Mike about Parker and his filth. For all her common-sense and talks with Faye, she still felt stupidly guilty. Could she have stopped it happening, or going so far? To control the shivers those thoughts began she sorted her clothes and packed at a rapid rate, then dumped her bags on the floor. She was ready to go.

A glance out of the window brought her back to the present and how near she had been to getting killed... Realistic, horrifying pictures of the times she had been out alone, vulnerable to the madman, raced through her mind. Had that stone, or whatever, that had whizzed past her yesterday, been meant to hit her? She remembered the crash as it hit a tree just beyond her. It had been going at a terrific rate and could have done real damage. Oh, dear Lord, the times she had put herself at his mercy...

Ashamed of her earlier suspicions of Mike, she gathered her things and went down.

'OK?'

'I'll be better when we leave here.'

'Pete's been on, and he's arranged an airlift.'

'A what?'

'A helicopter will be here in about fifteen minutes.'

'Thank goodness!' Oh, the relief. She could see herself being snatched up to safety, leaving the mad creature alone on the island. Then another thought struck her.

'What if he – the madman – tries to stop us?' she said. 'It would be easy enough if he has a weapon or something...'

'That's true, but if he had some sort of weapon, like a gun, then no doubt he would have shot at you instead of dropping boulders.' Again the voice of reason helped.

To make the time go, she plumped up cushions and straightened things while Mike raked the neglected fire and set the guard. Then they both had nothing to do but listen for the approach of the helicopter.

'You know, I really thought it was you I was seeing, despite never seeing his face and the hood always up. He kept making sure I saw him, then running off and hiding. Well, that's what it looked like. Now, I don't know.'

His dark eyebrows were drawn together, then he grinned and somehow managed to look contrite at the same time. 'I suppose it isn't surprising you didn't tell me after that first time when I as good as said your eyesight was defective.'

They both heard the helicopter at the same time. Their eyes and bodies alert, they rushed to the window. Yes, it was landing and in no time they had left the cottage, Mike calling, 'Go on,' to her as he stopped to double lock the sturdy door.

A figure in flying gear had jumped out and, bent double, was signing for them to do the same, but hurry to the machine.

Heart pumping madly, Sam was given a leg up inside, followed by Mike and the bags, then the navigator, and they were in the air.

Twisting round to view the island from the two hundred and forty degrees of the huge, glass bubble, Sam let out a cry when she saw a figure in a dark anorak running along the cliff edge. He was waving what looked like a crossbow in one hand and dangling something black and long in the other. He was obviously shouting at them.

'You're OK now,' the navigator said. 'He can't reach you.'

'What was that thing?'

'Looked to me like a crossbow and he was holding a dead bird by the neck,' their rescuer answered.

Sam shuddered and found herself gathered into Mike's strong arms.

'We're going to my place to finish the book.'

She was too relieved to be leaving Maidens Island to care if he was instructing, instead of asking. And his place in the Midlands would be better than being in the Bristol area.

Pete was standing beside his car when the helicopter landed and came forward to meet them as they jumped out.

'Are you OK, Sam?' He gathered her into a big brotherly hug. 'Faye sends her love and she'll phone you tomorrow.'

As they got in the car he said, 'Funny old business, but the police will go over first thing and round up your weirdo. They think it is probably someone who's flipped and is acting out Rambo fantasies.'

When they were on their way, Sam leaned forward. 'The police will tell us when they've found out who it is, won't they?' She needed to know for her own peace of mind.

'Yes. They reckon they should be able to tie it up by mid-morning tomorrow. Incidentally, Mike, that wooden boat you saw on the beach is probably one wrenched from its moorings up the coast somewhere. The one reported missing was a biggish inflatable. Its outboard was taken as well–'

Sam gasped. 'I saw an inflatable with an outboard in front of one of the cottages the other day.' Then, 'No, it was yesterday, I think.'

She shook her head, confused for the moment. 'Time is all shot to pieces. I'm not sure what day it is. So much seems to have happened in the last twenty-four hours.'

Pete grinned over his shoulder, but Mike said, 'Don't worry, life will slip back into routine in no time. And here we are. Home.'

Sam saw a big house across the winter-soaked lawn as the car drove round the semi-circular drive, then stopped in front of the rather grand oak door.

'It's beautiful, Mike.'

'Thank you.' He sounded pleased with the sincerity in her voice. 'But come in and get warm.'

He took her arm with rather old-fashioned courtesy and led her up the shallow steps and into a big square, oak-panelled hall. Pete followed with their bags, putting them down by the bottom of the carved staircase, and the brothers smiled their almost identical smiles as they watched her enjoyment of the house.

'It might be full of old, elegant charm,' Pete said, 'but thank goodness there's nothing old about your central heating, Mike. I've been very comfortable here.'

As he spoke they went past the open door of a very comfortable looking sitting-room, and a large, modern kitchen. The hefty, solid wood table and six matching chairs were divided from the work area, but still part of the whole.

Sam turned to Pete and said, 'This is surely what Faye is looking for?'

'Yes. It's Faye's dream to find a house like this somewhere close to Bristol. She came up at the week-end and went back with renewed fervour.'

Sam laughed. 'I can imagine.'

'I've got the house, but you're ahead of me with the family, Bruv,' Mike quipped. 'I'm looking to catch up in the near future, so you'd better help Faye with the house hunting.'

Sam could hear the childhood rivalry as the brothers teased one another, but when Pete tried to draw his brother out about the future Mrs Mike Manley, Mike only grinned and put his finger across his lips. Sam couldn't help wondering who the lucky lady might be. His publisher friend, Barbara? Whoever it was, she hoped the woman was worthy of him.

The next morning, Sam was surprised to find she had slept soundly, waking at her usual seven o'clock. She couldn't help a self-derisory grin – obviously, she felt safe here with two big men in the house to protect her!

Showering in her en-suite bathroom, she dried and dressed in her usual jeans and sweater, then went downstairs.

Breakfast was a light-hearted meal, cooked and served by both Mike and Pete and she enjoyed their familiar brotherly banter. Then Mike said, 'Heavy snow is forecast for later today, so Pete has decided to go back to Bristol this morning.'

'I don't want Faye going into the office in Bristol because I'm up here. And you know Faye – a bit of snow won't put her off trying to get the job done.'

Sam agreed with him.

'Mrs Bolton, my housekeeper, will be here before we go and I'll be back before she leaves,' Mike said. 'Will you be all right? Or would you prefer to come into the office with us?'

'Of course, I'll be OK here. I can get on as usual.'

They heard the outside door open into the scullery, then the housekeeper popped her head into the kitchen. Her face lit with surprise to see both Manley brothers and Sam, but after introducing Sam, Mike told her that he had decided The Manor was a more comfortable place to work.

Sam went with them to the front door giving Pete messages for her friend as he said goodbye and kissed her cheek. Mike grinned and did the same leaving her smiling at them both and waving them down the drive. She closed the door on the lowering skies and went into the office to get on with Jenny's story.

Poor Jenny, the beast of a man she lived with seemed to hold some fascination over her. She kept their home together when he was in jail for several months for receiving stolen goods, and she was there for him when he came out. But his gratitude, if he felt any, was short-lived and Jenny was soon battered and bruised again, but she stayed with him.

Sam's ire rose and she had to restrain herself, before she remembered the poor girl was dead. It was too late. She had wanted to take the girl in hand; tell her to get out, leave the swine.

She sat back in her chair feeling drained. It was a powerful story and Mike's girlfriend, Barbara, was right, people would want to read it. The more she read, the more she understood his frustration and why he needed to write the story.

Mrs Bolton came in with coffee and biscuits, remarking as she went out that the clouds were heavy with snow. Looking out the window Sam saw that the weather forecast was about to come true. She hoped Pete was well on his way back to Faye and turned to get on with her work.

'Faye's on the phone for you,' Mrs Bolton called round the door. Sam had not heard it ring, then when she looked round to pick it up there wasn't one in the room. She hurried along to the kitchen.

'Hi, Faye, how are you?'

'How are you, is more to the point,' Faye said.

'I'm fine, thanks, but – er – I'll be able to

tell you more later. Er, you know Pete is coming home today, don't you?' she stalled.

Sam felt awkward. Mike's housekeeper was busy in the kitchen and she did not like to discuss what was also his business in front of her. She had noted that he did not tell Mrs Bolton the real reason for his return.

'Do I take it you have company and can't talk?'

'That's right, Faye. I'll be in touch later, and thanks for calling.'

Feeling horribly frustrated because she needed to talk to her friend, she went back to the office and had a proper look for the telephone. She didn't find one, but she did find the set that recharged Mike's portable. When he was home he obviously kept it there. She went on with her typing.

'I've set soup and sandwiches in the kitchen, m'dear,' Mrs Bolton said, breaking through Sam's concentration. 'I'm afraid I'm going to have to leave. This snow really means business and if I don't go now, I can see me being stranded. You will explain to Mr Manley for me, won't you? Not that he'll need explanations, he's a good man and he'll understand. 'Bye for now, hope to see you tomorrow.'

She was gone almost before Sam could wish her a safe journey, and the house seemed suddenly very quiet, and very large.

Without thinking, Sam went through to the kitchen, then to the scullery to turn the key and slip the bolts on the back door. She could hear her mother saying, 'A sign of the times, having to lock yourself in your own home.' But then, Mum's garden backed on to open fields and some houses had been robbed while the owners were watching TV. This place was even worse, set, as it was, in the middle of nowhere, Sam justified her actions as she became aware of the absolute silence. Then she told herself she was a fool; when snow was falling in the countryside there was always this feeling of heavy silence.

Going to the kitchen window she saw, beyond the brick outbuildings, the vegetable garden smothered already, the few winter cabbages mere humps under the white blanket. The open countryside beyond the garden was no longer there, only the fat white and grey feathers falling relentlessly. No wonder Mrs Bolton had gone while the roads were still passable.

There was no point in worrying about Mike getting home. He would get here if it was at all possible. But the sky outside the window was black with snow. Odd how snow looked black when you looked up into the sky.

The smell of oxtail soup simmering on the stove reminded her it was past lunchtime and ladling some into a bowl she ate it, glad of something to do to break the quiet. The soup was delicious and if Mrs Bolton had made it, she was a treasure.

The phone rang and expecting it to be Mike, she eagerly plucked the receiver from the wall.

'Mike?' No reply. 'Mike?' she repeated. Still nothing; no dialling tone – not even heavy breathing. She nearly laughed out loud at the silly thought, then dropped the instrument as a deep male voice breathed, 'Hello ... o...'

She grabbed up the receiver and hung it back on the rest, standing shaking beside it. It rang again immediately, she plucked it up and put it straight back, then lifted it off again, not wanting to, but needing to check the dialling tone was there. It was. She let the receiver hang on its wire.

At least it couldn't be the madman from Maidens – it couldn't. He couldn't know where she would be. It was just a nuisance call. There were enough cranks about these days. But she wished Mike would come home soon, even though Pete, last night, had laughingly said this place was like Fort Knox. It was very big and she had just realised how dark inside it was with the snow blotting out the daylight. She turned all the lights on, then turned them all off. With the lights on, anybody outside would be able to see in easier and know she was alone.

The madman had found her on Maidens. It was not impossible to think he had found her again.

A high-pitched noise burst into the tense stillness – she jumped near out of her skin – it was the phone again. Probably someone trying to get through and she was being told her receiver was off the hook! Well, too bad!

Suppose it was Mike trying to tell her he couldn't get back? She dithered for another moment, then put the phone back and jumped as it warbled almost before she let go, then she had to decide whether to answer it.

She picked it up holding it away from her ear. 'Sam? Sam?'

'Mike?'

'Got you at last. I'm phoning from the car. I'll be home in a few minutes. If Mrs Bolton hasn't gone yet, she would be better staying with us.'

Relief surged through her.

She could see the drive from her room and she went up the stairs two at a time, switching the hall and landing lights on as she went, then her own bedside lamp. She positioned herself at the window in time to see the Range Rover turn steadily into the drive and go on round to the back of the house.

A bit breathless from her dash downstairs, Sam hurried through the kitchen switching on lights and going into the scullery – did she scream out loud? She wanted to, yet she was transfixed in the doorway. The toes of a pair of men's shoes lit by the kitchen light were sticking out under the curtain.

Someone was inside the house.

CHAPTER SIX

Sam couldn't take her eyes off the shoes – couldn't move. Hammering on the door distracted her for a second, then Mike was shouting, 'Sam, Sam, for goodness' sake, open the door.'

Avoiding the curtain she made a frantic scramble to the door, turned the key and released the bolts, then fell into Mike's arms, but with one hand over his mouth, she pointed soundlessly at the shoes.

'Hey, come on now,' he placated, holding her tight, and at the same time he pulled the curtain aside to reveal a pair of empty, old shoes in front of a pair of wellingtons and a couple of waterproofs hanging on hooks. 'I do occasionally do some gardening. But the fancy curtain came with the house and Mrs Bolton always draws it across. I usually leave it open.'

He pulled a face, trying to lighten her feeling of foolishness.

'How could I be that stupid?' She pulled herself away from him.

'Don't be so hard on yourself, Sam. You've had a lot to put up with lately.'

'Pete told you about Parker?'

'Who?'

'My ex-boss.'

'No, he didn't.' He paused. 'Is there something I should know?'

Sam shook her head. 'It's nothing.' But she reached up and bolted, then locked the door.

'I meant the traumas on Maidens. But you know, Pete was right when he said this place is a bit like Fort Knox. I don't think anyone is likely to get in, unless we let them in through the door.'

'That's a relief,' she said. 'Because someone, a man, phoned earlier. All he said was hello, but his voice... It was horrible...' Sam shuddered.

'No wonder you were jumpy. And no wonder you took the phone off the hook.' He looked fierce for a minute, then smiled. 'At least there's one good thing… You didn't think it was me!'

'Oh, Mike,' she said, but a lightness lifted her mood. It was relief that she was no longer alone in the big house, but she was honest enough to admit to herself that it was specially good having Mike's company.

When they walked into the kitchen she laughed as he sniffed the air.

'You look like the old adverts with the Bisto kids. Sit down and I'll heat some of Mrs Bolton's soup. It's delicious. Here, make a start on the rolls if you're as hungry as you look.'

He sat down at the table using her side plate for his roll and despite the nasty fright she had just given herself, the feeling of cosy domesticity was very pleasant.

While he ate his soup, Mike told her about the chaos in the city. Offices and shops were shutting so their staff could get home.

'And, I can tell you, I was relieved to see the gates here.' His smile was tender as he admitted, 'Knowing someone was waiting for me was kinda nice, too.'

A warm feeling spread through her, but not wanting to read the wrong things in his words, she said, 'I suppose you must rather rattle in this big place on your own.'

'Yes, I could do with someone to share it with.' He looked at her across the table, an unreadable expression on his face. Again, she did not quite know what to say, then was glad she hadn't said anything. 'Pete says I should get a dog.'

'What sort of dog? A guard dog? Or a pet?'

'I'd want one to be both.' A little frown clouded his face and Sam waited. 'We always said we would get another dog when we grew up, but neither of us has.' He stood up. 'Tea?' He filled the kettle as he carried on talking.

'Our dog escaped the crash with Pete and me, then, poor old thing, ran into another lorry swerving to avoid us and was killed.'

Sam's distressed gasp stopped him and he looked at her pale face.

'Didn't you know about the crash? I thought Faye must have told you.'

Sam shook her head. He made their tea and brought it to the table and sat down again.

'We were fourteen years old. Jake, our Irish Setter, was five. We were on our way home from holiday. Pete and I were asleep in the back of the car when a lorry jack-knifed in front of us. They said Dad managed to brake and so lessened the impact, but he and Mum were killed outright. We weren't injured.'

'Poor little boys.' For all he spoke matter of factly, Sam's heart ached for them.

'It's a long time ago, Sam. And we were not so little. Two hefty great lads our grand-ma used to call us.'

'So you went to live with your grand-mother? Thank heavens.'

'Well, no. Although she wanted us to, but, you see, Grandad had had a stroke and she had enough to cope with looking after him.

We compromised, Pete and I went into care not far from Gran's and we were able to help her and Grandad. And Tom and Mary, our house parents, were great, so you see we were very lucky.'

'There aren't many would say that–'

'Ah, but, Pete and I knew how lucky we were. We had had loving parents and grandparents and all our memories were good. And there were lots of them.' He looked directly at her. 'Some of the other poor devils in our home would have had difficulty dredging up just one, believe me.'

'Oh, Mike,' she choked, shaking her head to clear the shimmer of tears at the thought of such unhappiness. He came round the table and, wiping her eyes with his handkerchief, pressed her head against him, gently smoothing her hair.

'I suppose that is one of the reasons I wanted to write the book. Apart from feeling guilty that I failed Jenny.' Mike hugged her tight, then moved away. 'Let's go into the sitting-room.' He picked up their mugs and led the way out of the kitchen.

Putting her tea on a little table beside a comfortable, fireside chair, he bent down and depressed a switch. The log fire flamed instantly to life and Mike sat on the big sofa near to Sam.

'No driftwood, I'm afraid, only gas.'

'I can still enjoy the effect and imagine it's real,' she told him. 'But, carry on about Jenny – that's if you want to...'

After a pause he said, 'You were right, the fictional Tony is me, but Jenny is her real name.' A furrow creased his forehead. 'She was such a pathetic, little creature when she first came to the home, but she blossomed like a flower when anyone was kind to her. Pete and I were the oldest, so it was not surprising that she came to us with any problems. Usually me...'

His lips twisted into a memory-filled smile. 'Because I am fifteen minutes older than him, Pete called me Big Bruv, and Jenny needed a big brother. The poor kid took some time before she trusted adults, but

Tom and Mary were terrific people and won her round.'

He stopped and sat looking at the flames licking the artificial logs.

'What happened when you left the home?'

'Grandad died just before we were sixteen and we went to live with Grandma, but, we kept in touch with Tom and Mary and knew that Jenny was all right. We both felt a responsibility for her somehow.'

He got up and went over to the window.

'Is it still snowing?'

'No, it's stopped, but I'll have to dig the car out before I put it in the garage.'

He drew the curtains and switched on a couple of table lights, then turned the main light off, leaving a soft comfortable glow before he sat down again.

'Jenny was all right until she left Tom and Mary's and was persuaded by a friend to go to London.' He looked at Sam and shook his head unhappily. 'It's a sad fact that girls with Jenny's background often choose the wrong men. Jim isn't his real name, but– He knocked her about. But you know all this, don't you?'

'Go on,' she urged, knowing he needed to talk about it.

Mike took her hand in his and gave it a gentle squeeze. 'When she left him after several bad beatings and twice went to one of the women's sheltered houses, he talked her into going back to him again.'

'I have heard that is fairly common,' Sam said.

Mike nodded. 'Yes, but when she found she was pregnant, Jenny ran away up here to me. I think she would have had a complete breakdown had I not taken her in. Even so she was terrified he would find her and talk her into going back to him. It was her baby she was scared for – she'd already miscarried once after he used her as punchbag.'

Sam could feel the tension in his hand, though he did not transfer it to crush her own.

'Poor Jenny.'

Sam sat in the long silence wondering

what made women cling to such rotten men. She knew she would move heaven and earth to get away, rather than give any man the chance of a second thump. Then she looked at Mike and tried to imagine the dilemma he had found himself in. He was leaning forward, fascinated by the shimmering flickers of the flaming logs as he rested his loosely clasped hands on his knees.

'I told her the one way for her to be safe was for us to get married. If she was my wife, he would know he couldn't persuade her to go back.'

Sam found her jaw had dropped open when he sat up and turned to look straight into her eyes. She closed her mouth.

His face was taut with painful memories. 'I was wrong!'

She, who, before meeting Mike Manley, was never at a loss for words, was once more speechless.

Mike married? Instantly she remembered that Jenny was dead. Poor Mike. Obviously he had always loved Jenny. It must have hurt like the very devil to hear how she had been treated, and, worse, had gone back to the same man for more.

'I'm sorry, Mike. You must have loved her very much.' She reached over and covered his hand with hers.

'No-one could help loving Jenny.' He gave her a faint smile, then Sam's breath stopped as their eyes met and it was as though neither could look away.

The phone shrilled on a small table by the window and Sam wanted to shout, not now!

'It'll be Pete, I should think,' Mike said, striding across the room to answer it.

It was Pete and though she wanted to speak to Faye, she did not want to talk to her friend with Mike there.

'Pete is home safe and sound. Driving conditions were pretty hazardous, though as he drove south the snow stopped, the roads were icy and treacherous. Faye will give you a ring tomorrow.' He delivered the message as he replaced the receiver, but before she could move, the phone rang again.

Split-second thinking quelled her urge to tell him not to answer it, it would be a good thing for a heavy breather to hear there was a man in the house. It was not a nuisance call.

'That was the police,' Mike said coming back to his seat. 'They've been across to the island – no snow there – and neither was our unwelcome visitor. He had broken into several of the other houses, but there wasn't much damage and, naturally, the boat and outboard had gone as well. It was probably, as they said, some nut acting out his fantasies and when he saw you there, tried to scare you off so he could have the place to himself.'

'I hope they're right, but I'm sorry they didn't catch him.'

Later, in her bedroom, she pulled the elegant, corded drapes apart. She liked to see when it was light in the morning and, ignoring the fact that it was winter and would be dark until late, she always performed the nightly ritual.

The snow showed up the whole garden and she could see as far as the high wall and open gate. Conifers like tall, black sentinels curved with the drive, the nearly full moon in the clear cold sky casting their shadows across the smooth unbroken white blanket. Then, as she watched, the moon disappeared behind long straggling clouds and the charming scene was suddenly full of menace. The conifers no longer guarding were now threatening. Sam shivered and got back into bed.

Luxuriating in the warm kitchen while she waited for the kettle to boil next morning, Sam was not really surprised when the phone rang.

'Hi, Sam. What excitement, eh?' Faye's expected voice sang down the line. They were both early risers and since meeting up again they often had an early chat. 'Or was it exciting?'

'I'm not sure,' Sam said. 'The helicopter ride was OK, but that weirdo on the island – no!' She took a deep breath and told her friend what the police had said. 'He probably thought no-one else would be there at this time of year. Mike thinks that's the last we'll hear of him, too.'

'But you don't, do you, Sam?'

'Oh, Faye. No, I don't.' She stopped for a few seconds, glad of her friend's understanding as she picked up her anxiety. 'I think Parker has hired someone to frighten me, perhaps, hurt me, just to show he's not beaten.' Sam heard Faye's gasp. 'I know it sounds far-fetched, but that man is evil, Faye.'

'I believe you, love. Don't you worry, Pete and Mike will sort him out–'

'Not Mike. I haven't said anything about Parker to him and I'd rather he didn't know.'

'If you say so, Sam, but Pete will go and see Parker and let him know that we know what he is up to. Anyway, from the pictures of your snow on TV, Mike could have a job getting down to Bristol for quite some time.'

Sam told her how deep the snow was. 'The house looks as though it is sitting in the middle of a huge, smooth tub of sparkly ice-cream.'

Faye groaned. 'Thank goodness I've stopped the morning sickness. The thought of so much ice-cream is enough to start it off again. Mike is thinking of getting married so Pete says, but he doesn't know who to, though. Mike's a super guy, isn't he? He deserves a nice girl. Pete says I mustn't matchmake, but he'll make someone a good husband – if only he could stop feeling so guilty about Jenny.'

'I don't think you need worry. From what he's said, I agree with Pete. I think there is someone already.'

'Oh?'

Had she said too much? 'I could be wrong, of course. She may be just a business friend.'

'Don't worry, Sam, I won't say anything. I'll only tell Pete you think that guy on the island was sent by Parker. He'll make sure Parker stops the man straight away, or suffer the consequences.'

A great weight, that she hadn't known was there, lifted from her shoulders and Sam could breathe more easily after she put the phone down. Faye and Pete were good friends.

Mike arrived in the kitchen in time to catch the toast before it went up in flames. Sam watched as he scraped the burned crumbs into the sink.

'Yuk!'

He turned round with a quizzical frown.

'I can't think how I ever thought you were a tidiness freak,' Sam commented.

'Me?' He obviously knew his faults.

'Yes. Remember when I first arrived at Maidens? You showed me the bathroom and told me not to touch your things?' She kept a stern frown and saw he did remember. 'I wondered what sort of man I was working for when I saw everything set out with surgical precision. And to be warned off touching them?'

She grinned then and shook her head. 'Didn't last, did it? I soon found you were

111

an untidy so and so.'

'I like a few things about – makes a place feel like home,' he protested, though his eyes were smiling. He put the scraped toast in the rack. 'We don't know how long we're likely to be marooned, so we'll have to preserve rations.'

'Dear me, life with you, Mike Manley, is never dull, is it? After suffering raging storms, a mad man and a helicopter rescue from a wild Welsh island, I'm marooned in the middle of the country by freak snow conditions and in danger of starving to death.' She pulled an impish face at him. 'And I won't be able to go out for my walk this afternoon.'

'Why not?'

'I've nothing to wear.'

Mike laughed out loud at the age-old feminine cry, then eyed her up carefully. 'I think I can find something suitable for madame.'

A tiny frisson of – she didn't know what – but something made her cold as she waited to refuse the offer of his girlfriend's clothes.

'I'm almost sure Faye said she was leaving her ski stuff behind when they went to Bristol,' Mike continued. 'They went for an early ski-trip before they moved.'

Fortunately Faye had salopettes, as well as a ski suit, and Sam, being shorter and, before Faye's pregnancy, rounder than her friend was able to wear those with her own anorak. Several pairs of socks made the snow boots a reasonable fit and she went to join Mike outside the back door.

'That's it, I'm ready. But–'

'But what?' Mike asked, looking at her quizzically.

'Which way are we going?' Then she rushed on, 'I know I'm a fool, but I don't want to walk down the drive.'

'We're going the back way. Is that OK?'

Sam nodded. 'I just didn't want to spoil that beautiful picture at the front. Not even birds have been on it, you know.'

Mike laughed. 'I thought everyone wanted to walk in virgin snow and leave their own tracks.'

'Yes, that's true, I do usually. But the front garden looks so lovely – pure white with the dark green trees.'

He smiled his understanding and they set off, managing the deep snow quite well.

Once away from the garages and out-buildings, the snow was much deeper, above Sam's knees and she was soon having a job, lifting each leg up and over, just to move forward.

'I suppose it is funny to watch me struggling,' she said, trying to sound severe, but failing. She picked up a handful of snow and, moulding it, threw the snowball at her amused companion.

'Lucky hit,' he called, moving away as fast as his long legs would go through the snow. A few yards away he turned with a snowball all ready to aim – she ducked and laughed at him.

'Rotten shot!' she shouted, taunting him with another well-aimed hit.

In no time the years had vanished and she was a child again.

'Pax!' Mike called eventually, holding his arms aloft, showing empty hands. 'Wow, you're a real wild cat when you get going, aren't you? Poor brothers...'

'Poor nothing! How do you think I learned to look after myself? They treated me like another brother.'

'Ah,' he said knowingly.

Without question they left the battlefield of trampled snow and carried on across open parkland. The countryside stretched out before them smooth, brilliant white, sparkling in the sunshine; the occasional tall tree breaking the pattern of white humps marking the distant hedges.

After waiting for Sam a couple of times Mike said, 'It might be easier if you follow in my steps – touch of the Wenceslas and page?'

'Certainly, your Majesty,' Sam said, bowing and stepping into his tracks. It was a bit easier for her, but after the snowball fight and fighting to get through the snow, she was not disappointed when Mike stopped and she looked up to see the back of the house quite nearby.

'Did you realise we were so near?' Mike asked her.

'No. We must have come in a circle.'

'That's right, and just in time if this sky is as full of snow as it looks.'

It was and their tracks had been covered when Sam looked out of the back door next morning. Delighted to be 'marooned' again, she got two mugs down, sure Mike would be in the office.

She reached for the kettle when a movement through the window caught her eye.

Mike came running at her shout and she pointed to the long, black thing swinging in the wind.

It was a dead bird...

CHAPTER SEVEN

Mike rushed through the scullery and she heard him open the back door. Suppose whoever put that thing there was waiting? To do what, she chided herself, and instantly remembered the crossbow.

'Mike,' she bawled, dashing after him. He was closing the back door.

'Sit down, Sam,' he said. 'It must have been put there before the last snow fell. There are no footprints just dents in the snow so whoever is playing games will be long gone.'

Shuddering, she recalled, 'It was a dead cormorant we saw from the helicopter, wasn't it?'

'Afraid so,' he said. 'It's got to be the same person.'

'That means he could have a crossbow,

doesn't it?'

'Yes, very probably.'

'And we might think we're marooned, but he isn't, is he? So who is it, Mike? Who would know where I am? After all, I don't really know where I am – just that I'm in your house, in the country near Birmingham...'

She was feeling badly shaken and welcomed Mike's arm round her shoulders and his caring hug.

'I'm sorry, Sam, but I can only guess who it might be. The fact that he's followed us here could make it easier to fathom.' A deep frown creased his face. 'I'll have a word with Ken Preston, an old friend in the police. Come on, we'll be more comfortable in the sitting-room.'

Sam went very willingly.

He turned on the log fire, gave her hands a reassuring squeeze, then picked up the phone.

As he was getting through, Sam tried to dispel images of the madman waving crossbow and dead bird as they soared away to safety. Safety? Where was safety? What had happened to her ordinary, reasonably happy life?

'Ken? Mike Manley. Ken, can you give me any more information on Frank Ross?'

Sam watched as Mike listened, his face fierce.

'Pete's told you about the idiot on Maidens, hasn't he? It could be Frank... But whoever it is, he's turned up here and left a calling card.'

Mike finished his call. 'Frank Ross apparently dropped out of sight two or three weeks ago,' he told her. 'I don't really think it is him, but he's capable of all sorts. I'll make that cup of tea.'

When he had gone Sam tried to think how she could get out of this mess, but Mike was back before she had one decent idea.

'I'm afraid I've spoiled your virgin drive,' he said giving her a mug of tea. 'I went out and had a look around, but from what I can make out, someone came up to the house, via the back of the trees, before the last snow stopped.'

Sam swallowed hard and composed herself as Mike sat down.

'I – I'm not sure, Mike, but I might know who it is.'

He looked at her sharply. It was only right that she should tell him. He was as involved almost as much as she was. Well, he had to deal with her panicky moments.

She gave him a crooked little grimace. 'I think it is my ex-boss – trying to frighten me.' Then, gripping her mug in both hands, she drank deeply.

'Do you want to tell me why you think he would do that?' When she hesitated he said, 'You can't go through life allowing someone to scare you like this.' He took her mug and put it in the hearth, then took her hands in his. 'I'd like to help you, Sam. Won't you trust me?'

'Of course I trust you,' she burst out. 'Whatever makes you think I don't?'

'You didn't trust me on Maidens,' he

stated baldly. 'And you didn't like it when you thought Pete had told me about your ex-boss.' His head tipped to one side and his lips twisted. 'The guy must be some weirdo.'

She wanted to tell him about Parker, but she didn't want him to think badly of her.

'I was Parker's personal assistant, so naturally, I had to work closely with him. I soon saw how efficiently he put the boot in if someone bested him. I didn't like the man, but when he first touched me, he did it in such a way I wasn't sure if it was accidental!'

She stopped and searched for the right words, glad when Mike didn't say anything.

'He obviously thought I enjoyed his attentions and he became really foul. Naturally I told him what he could do with his job, even threatened him with the Tribunal, but he assured me no-one would believe me against him, nor would I get another job. He's powerful, and he is vicious, and I was already looking for another job. I have a mortgage to pay.'

The flood of words stopped, but she still could not look at Mike, or she would have seen his fury. 'Pete and Faye told me about you needing someone. You know the rest.' She looked up this time. 'I really did try to stop him...'

'I know that.' His positive tone reassured her as nothing else could and he crouched down in front of her.

'Poor Sam, you have had a rotten time of it.'

His gentle, understanding words opened the flood gates and tears spilled down her cheeks.

'That's right, let it all out,' he soothed as he put his arms around her and held her tenderly. When she started to sniff, they both searched pockets for a handkerchief and suddenly life was back to normal; they grinned as each produced a crumpled, soft, cotton hankie.

Mike wiped her wet face and told her, 'Some men like it when a woman says no. It sounds as though your ex-boss is one of them. They are quite often ineffectuals who see women as a way to dominate.'

He laughed at Sam's amazement with this character reading. 'I did psychology as a second degree and I guess some of it stuck,' he excused. 'Damn this snow. As soon as I can get down there, I'll make sure he never bothers you again, Sam.'

She sat up. 'Er – Pete is going to see him–'

'Pete knew it was him? Why didn't he say?'

'He didn't know – that is, he'll know now because Faye will have told him.' She repeated what she had told Faye over the phone.

'So that's why you didn't recognise the lunatic on Maidens? It wasn't Parker himself?'

'Oh, no, he's too old and too fat to be running about on an island, let alone heaving boulders. And I can't see him venturing out in deep snow, either.'

Mike bunched his hands into fists as he said grittily, 'Between us, Pete and I will make sure he knows to call off his hired help and forget any idea of revenge.' He stood up. 'Will you be all right? I'll get on to Pete and see what he's doing about Parker.'

He went out and it said much for Sam's state of mind that she didn't notice he'd ignored the phone on the table, preferring to use the mobile.

'Pete? Sam's has just told me about Parker. The swine.'

'He's all of that, Bruv,' Pete said, and heard the intense anger as Mike told him about the dead cormorant on the garage wall and Sam's frightening phone call.

'I should think poor old Sam was scared to death. But I'm just off to see Parker at his office; I want to be waiting when he arrives. He was out when I went along yesterday. Want me to do anything different?'

'This blasted snow! I'd like to sort him out. He'd think twice before messing about with another girl, then terrifying her,' he grated. 'But even if the thaw is as rapid as they say, I can't see me getting away from here before tomorrow. Anyway, until Parker calls off his idiot, I can't think of leaving Sam on her own. She's being brave, but obviously she has reason to know Parker is a vengeful devil. Has to be to hire a madman to do his dirty work.'

Mike listened to his brother's choice words describing Parker, then said, 'Did I tell you the police found a dead bird hanging from a crossbow bolt on the cottage door? Whoever did it has got to be mad. I haven't told Sam about that. She was upset enough when she saw the idiot chasing the helicopter with one.' After another angry expletive, Mike said, 'I could walk into town and get a train down, but Sam couldn't.'

'Don't you worry, Mike, I'll make sure Parker knows he's hog-tied if he tries to play games with me.'

Pete silently thanked the snow for keeping Mike away from Parker right now. It had been a while since he'd heard such aggressive noises from his brother.

'Ken Preston says Frank Ross dropped out of sight almost as soon as he came out, but I agree that this job does sound more like Parker than him. Still, I'll let you know when I locate him. It will be as well to know where Ross is, now he's on the streets again.'

Ken Preston was an old friend and was now Detective Inspector Preston. They had all grown up knowing who the local petty villains were and Frank Ross had been one of them before going to London. The fact that Jenny had lived with Ross for years interested the police greatly when she had died under the London Tube train, but Frank Ross had been elsewhere at the time, and was subsequently sent to prison. He served the full five years of his sentence and that said a lot for his behaviour inside.

Ken Preston knew the Manley brothers' connection with Jenny and had told them when Ross was about to be released.

Sam was watching the impotent flames' relentless effort to devour the artificial logs when Mike went back into the sitting-room. She looked really fed up.

'Pete has everything in hand,' he told her

cheerfully. 'Parker won't trouble you again, Sam. But I'm afraid I'm going to need some typing done, if this manuscript is to be ready for my editor on time.'

She jumped up, ashamed that she had allowed a lump of depression to settle on her while Mike was out of the room.

'I'll be glad to get back to the book,' she said lightly, then wondered if that was the most tactful thing to say. When all was said and done, Jenny had been going to be Mike's wife, and now she was dead.

Poor Jenny continued between a rock and a hard place, desperate for any small amount of affection Jim might show her, but always in a state of anxiety in case she got pregnant.

The torment, anguish and desperation were captured for all to read as Sam, tears running down her own cheeks, rapidly typed the story. She hoped she would never come face to face with this Jim, for she was not sure what she would do to him.

When, pregnant once again, Jenny fled

with only the clothes she was dressed in, she phoned Tony from Birmingham station in a shocking state. She told him she was going to hide in the Ladies' until he got there. She was pitifully afraid Jim might have followed her.

Tony had to ask a woman, a complete stranger, to go into the Ladies' Toilet and call out that Tony was here for Jenny. The motherly country woman did not ask questions, but her smile was sympathetic when she came out with the sickly pale Jenny who cried, 'Tony,' and threw herself into his arms.

Sam rushed on, keen to know if Jim had followed Jenny, but Tony brought the young girl home without encountering the irate boyfriend.

Then Sam found she was looking for signs of Mike/Tony showing his feelings, then asking Jenny to marry him. It was difficult to remember he was called Tony in the story, even though she was reading the name. Glancing up the screen she saw Mike's name and knew she would have to use the change facility when she came to the end. Goodness only knew how many times she had put the wrong name.

Sam came aware of her surroundings as she looked up and saw Mike watching her, dismay on his face.

She smiled and he said, 'That's better. I thought you'd been crying.'

She blinked her eyes. 'I think I have been. This is no Cinderella story, you know. It gets a bit too raw for comfort.'

'Hmm, I did have some doubts about you typing it.'

She looked at him in disbelief, then teased, 'Is that why George left?'

He grinned. 'No, though, to give him his due, he did find the beginning rather harrowing. No,' he repeated, 'I am why he left.'

'Good grief, what did you do?'

'I sometimes used his shaving gear for shaving and his towel to dry myself and he just could not take that. Said I was a hopeless case... And I didn't plump the cushions after sitting on the chairs... And I–'

'OK, I believe you. I have lived with you, too.' Then she remembered, 'Of course, it was George who left everything all tidy before leaving. I wish I'd known... That first sight of the bathroom on Maidens will live with me for ever.'

She shook her head and gave him an impudent grin as she took the mug of coffee he'd brought in.

'So you think the book is too much?'

'Definitely not, but it is powerful and not for the faint-hearted. And at the moment, I can only see an unhappy ending.' She waited for him to tell her she was wrong, but he didn't.

'That is one of my problems – the ending. But perhaps Barbara will be able to help me there.'

Sam didn't really want to hear about the wonderful Barbara but said, 'Do you mean you might manufacture an ending just to make it happy-ever-after stuff?'

'No, not that, but apparently publishers

want, if not happy or hopeful, a suitable come-uppance for the bad guy. That's why I am having difficulties. How do I show Tony getting his just desserts for failing Jenny? When not a lot has changed in my life – I'm not getting just desserts yet!'

'For heaven's sake, Mike. How can you be so stupid?' Exasperation raised her voice to a near shout. 'How can Tony be the bad guy? The man's a saint. Just think what he did for that little girl, then the young woman. How many men do you know who would have married someone who was carrying someone else's baby? Eh?' Her shoulders were heaving, then she remembered – Mike Manley and Tony were one and the same man. 'Oh, dear!'

They were both standing, but she didn't remember getting up.

'Oh, dear, indeed, Samantha Turner,' he said huskily as he swept her to him, his lips on hers as she opened her own for him to deepen the kiss. She'd come home. This was why she couldn't have stayed with Derek –

she had needed to find her soulmate. She strained nearer, the scent of him stirring her desire…

Suddenly the sound of the phone was intruding – she didn't want him to hear, to answer it. Alone she listened as he spoke to his brother – so much for twins knowing how the other was feeling!

That something was wrong was clear as Mike snapped out, 'What? Are you absolutely sure? Yes, yes, Pete, but – then who…?'

He listened again, and in the silence Sam's neck tensed – the horror was not over yet. 'I'll wait to hear from you. And thanks, Pete. Yes, as soon as…'

Mike came back to Sam and putting his arm round her led her back to the armchair. He sat on the chair arm when she was seated. 'I'm afraid, we're going to have to think again. Pete is one hundred per cent sure that this lunatic has nothing to do with Parker.'

CHAPTER EIGHT

Suddenly, Sam gasped and sat down. If it wasn't Parker then that left only one person.

'You've thought of someone else?'

'Derek – an old boyfriend. It's not long since we parted. He wasn't happy when I broke it off with him, but I don't really think he would go to such lengths. That would be far too uncivilised for Derek.'

'Better give me his name and address, and his work place, and I'll get Pete to check him out. We can't afford to miss anyone with the slightest reason for holding a grudge against you. Or against me, for that matter.'

Sam went back to her typing. Her mood vastly different now and she had typed the words without registering where Mike/Tony suggested Jenny marry him. When they finally impinged on her consciousness she went back to read the passage carefully.

It was a strange feeling, knowing it was Mike, though there was no emotion as such to tell her what Mike really felt about Jenny. It was probably too painful for him to put in the book, but she suspected Barbara would demand he put it in.

Turning back the cover to start on the last A4 manuscript pad, Sam wondered how much more of the story there was. She flipped over the pages and didn't know whether she was disappointed or pleased when there were only a few more hand-written sheets left to type. She got on as fast as she could, gripped by a peculiar sense of urgency.

Mike came into the office just as she finished typing the last of his writing.

'All done,' she told him.

'You don't sound too impressed, Sam.'

'I think most of it is excellent, but this last little bit is – well, it's almost noteform rather than a story. But you said the story is not finished, so that's probably why.'

'Yes, I want Barbara to read it through again before I write the ending.'

'Barbara? Lucky you, having a friend in publishing.'

'Yup. I'm looking forward to hearing what she says once she sees it again.'

Later, hearing Mike's happy laugh through the open office door, Sam smiled and paused at the bottom of the stairs.

He was speaking on the phone and before she could move away she heard the full-throated emotion as he said, 'Yes, Barbara, I couldn't have managed without you. I'm looking forward to that as well – who else could get me through this? And I'll be with you as soon as...'

Sam hurried into the sitting-room and closed the door. So now she knew. There was no mistaking – it was Barbara who was to be Mrs Mike Manley.

He was still smiling when he came into the room and Sam tried not to show her unhappy state, saying cheerfully, 'As soon as this snow allows, I'll get back to Bristol.'

'It's raining now,' Mike told her. 'The weatherman was right about a rapid thaw. I expect we'll be cut off by flooding next.'

She knew he was watching as she hurried across to the window.

'Good heavens, I've never seen deep snow go so fast,' she said, suddenly miserable. 'I should be able to get a taxi to the station later this afternoon if this keeps up,' she said. Looking at the torrential rain reminded her of her arrival on Maidens.

'Don't you think you'd be better staying here until we find out who this weirdo is – who and why?' His quiet voice of reason reminded her to get herself together.

'I'm an idiot. Of course, I'll feel safer here in your Fort Knox than my little flat.'

It was only then she noticed he had placed a bottle of champagne and two glasses on the table. Uncorking the bottle and pouring, he said, '"Jenny's Story" is ready to despatch, so I think we should celebrate. To you, Sam,' he said, raising his glass. 'My thanks for doing a really good job under very difficult conditions.'

She reciprocated making every effort to sound happy, 'To the success of "Jenny's Story."'

Sam was agreeably lighthearted throughout dinner as she enjoyed a second and third glass of the dry, bubbly wine.

Easy-going friendliness permeated the meal and afterwards they sat in front of the log fire reading, talking and listening to music. As the final strains of 'West Side Story' faded Mike said, 'Terrific. I could get used to spending my evenings like this, you know.'

'Mmm, yes, very pleasant,' she said, thanking the champagne for dulling the pain of 'if only.' If only he was not involved with Barbara...

Too tired almost to drag herself upstairs, she knew she must and wished him, 'Goodnight,' refusing his offer of brandy and went up to bed.

It was a pity that washing and cleaning teeth should waken you up before you got into bed she decided, but she turned the light off and opened her curtains, pleased to see the rain had stopped. The snow was almost gone and she looked across to the high conifers just as the clouds parted to reveal the full moon. The effect was nothing like the shadows on fresh snow – but what was that?

A narrow shape separated itself from the black tree nearest the house – it was a man – she saw the pale oval, his face, looking up. Frozen for a second she heard the thwack nearby and screamed as she fled from the room.

Outside her door she ran into Mike.

'What on earth?' He caught her in his arms. 'What is it? What happened?'

She held on to him as he tried to go into the room. Shaking violently, Sam forced the words out.

'Somebody shot at me – a bolt, I think. It hit the window frame.'

'Did it break the window? You're not hurt?' She shook her head at his rapid fire questions.

'But what if he breaks the windows downstairs and tries to get inside? What shall we do?'

Mike lifted her chin to look into her eyes. 'If the unlikely happens and he shows himself inside, then I'll deal with him.'

She already felt better, hearing his confident voice.

'But, I have taken the precaution of closing the downstairs shutters and they are all locked in place. So you see, it is very nearly impossible for anyone to get in. Does that help? Do you feel any safer? Mmm?'

'Do you mean you went outside and put shutters up?' She could not believe what she heard. 'Are you mad? Any – anything could have happened to you.'

Mike smiled at her horrified tone and shook his head. 'No, I didn't go outside. The shutters are inside. Here, like this.'

He went across to the landing window and lifted the wide, hinged sill, pulling the weighted wooden blind up to cover the window. Sam watched fascinated and felt relief warm her body.

'I've never seen inside shutters before. I didn't know they existed. You're right, I do feel safer…' She trailed off unhappily.

'But…?' He smoothed her hair away from her face. 'Come on, we'll ring the police. Not that they'll find much in the dark, but if the guy is hanging about, he'll think twice if he sees one or two police cars here.'

It felt good to know that several policemen had searched the grounds, even though they found no-one. Then forensic had taken the crossbow bolt from the window frame, promising, if there were fingerprints on it, they would soon have the villain. Sam and Mike finally said good-night to the last policeman.

'It's nearly three o'clock,' she said wearily.

Mike nodded and put his arm about her shoulders leading her out of the kitchen and switching off the light. Her feet dragged a bit the nearer she got to her own room and she knew Mike looked down into her face.

'Would you rather not sleep in there?'

Sam exhaled a deep breath. The shutters had been pulled up, she knew, but it took all her courage to say, 'I'll be fine, Mike. No problem.'

'Sure?'

'Yes, sure,' she said, not at all sure. 'Goodnight, or rather, good-morning.' She smiled to show him she was all right and went into the room. What else could she do?

Daylight was searching for a way in round the edge of the curtains when Sam blinked awake. It was not like her to forget to open them. Then full memory of the previous night cascaded over her. And, of course, it was dark – there were shutters at the windows.

When Sam went downstairs she was surprised to find two men in the kitchen with Mike.

They exchanged greetings and Mike introduced her to Detective Inspector Ken Preston and his detective constable.

'They have found a part-print on the bolt,

Sam,' Mike explained.

'Yes, and with today's computer search facility we should have a name soon,' Ken Preston added. 'That is, of course, if the villain is on file.' He stood up and thanked Mike for his tea, then, followed by his detective constable, went to take another look around outside.

'Egg? Bacon?' Mike asked, cracking an egg in the frying-pan beside the already cooking bacon.

'Please,' Sam said.

'Do you want to go back to Bristol? Or would you rather stay here?'

'Bristol.' The answer was quick but quiet, as Sam recalled the fright of the night before. She was honest enough to admit to herself that she would miss Mike, but if the lunatic was after her, and it looked very likely...

'I can't believe it's Derek doing this, but whoever it is knows I'm here, so it makes sense for me to leave.'

Truth to tell she wanted to disappear

before he did her real harm.

'I'll take you–'

'No! That is, thanks, but if he's watching, he might follow us. The Range Rover is too…' Sam sat back and shook her head. 'I don't know what to think, what to do.'

'Leave it for now. We might hear from Pete soon.'

There must be something about twins' thought transference after all, Sam supposed, when Pete rang a few minutes later.

Mike listened carefully, then told his brother he'd call back in five minutes.

'Your Derek is–'

'He's not mine.'

'True. Pete told me that Derek Granger is on honeymoon in St Lucia. He's moved from his flat to a rather grand townhouse where there's room for a nursery. Mrs Derek Granger is five months pregnant.' He paused. 'That doesn't sound to me as though he's bearing a grudge; but what do you think?'

'No. I'm sure he's very happy. He was

desperate for children, but I...' She tailed off, feeling terrible all over again.

'Hey, come on. He was obviously the wrong guy for you, Sam.'

How did he do it? Mike Manley could surely read her mind. But, no matter how, it soothed her guilty feelings.

Mike pulled her up and put his arms about her. 'You've been worrying in case it was him, haven't you?'

'Yes. I couldn't bear the thought of trusting someone and being so close for more than two years, then finding that I hadn't known him at all.'

Mike tightened his arms and laid his cheek on the top of her head. It was easier to carry on when she couldn't see his face.

'He – Derek said a few nasty things when I first broke off with him and we met in the lift – we worked in the same building – but... That's how I came to be working for Parker; I changed jobs to avoid him, I'm just glad it wasn't him.'

'I can understand that, though we are

144

rather left with a big blank again, aren't we? Are you sure there's no-one else you can think of? It might be someone who fancies you. That can happen. Seeing us together he could think we were lovers and he might prefer to harm you rather than let you be with someone else. Cast your mind over the last few months – possibly someone you worked with, or someone who worked with Derek. While you have a think, I'll phone Pete to let him know you're going back to Bristol.'

Left to herself, Sam tried really hard to conjure a face or a name that might fit Mike's theory, but when he returned she had to confess to utter failure.

'Pete says he's thinking of going into the private eye business if computer software fails. He's enjoyed snooping and has even come up with a fellow's whereabouts whom I thought could be involved. But Frank Ross doesn't know you, so when you leave here you'll be all right. He might be trying, in some twisted way, to pay me back, so the sooner you're on your way home, the better.'

'But—'

'But me no buts, lady. You have packing to do.'

She'd wanted to say, what about you, Mike? But he would not want to hear her fears, so she got on with her packing and carried it downstairs to be greeted by Mrs Bolton.

'What about that snow then?' The house-keeper, hardly pausing to say good-morning, told hoary tales of how each one of her family managed to survive the dreadful conditions.

'Thank you, Mrs Bolton,' Mike said. 'You did say you would make the policemen some coffee, didn't you?' When she had bustled off he said, 'Now, I think, in case the police haven't scared off our man, it would be as well if he doesn't see you leave.'

Sam nodded her complete agreement.

'I'll go into the office as usual – with the police here you'll be OK and I don't want him suspecting any deviation from normal.'

Sam was quite enthusiastic when Mike explained his plan.

It involved one of the policemen putting his head inside Mrs Bolton's car bonnet and leaving it up to show defeat. Poor Mrs Bolton was to stand beside her car in her hat and coat looking very worried. Later a taxi would take her home – except it would be Sam in the housekeeper's coat and hat and she was to be taken to the railway station...

As the train began to move, a well-dressed man scrambled aboard, taking the seat opposite Sam.

'Made it,' he said with an attractive grin.

Sam smiled and nodded, then went back to her newspaper. She was glad he did not try to start a conversation, but later when she'd finished the paper, she offered it to him.

'Thanks. I didn't get time to buy one.'

Sam read her paperback and in next to no time it seemed the train was pulling into Temple Meads Station.

'It worked like clockwork, Faye,' Sam said as her friend gave her an emotional hug when they met on the platform. 'It's good to be back in dear old Bristol. I never thought I'd say that!'

They climbed into a waiting taxi and Faye gave her address as they sat back. When they were inside her spacious apartment, Faye said, 'I'm so relieved you're home. Things seemed to be getting out of hand.'

'I'll say! I'm relieved, too. Or I would be if I knew Mike was all right.'

'Mike's gone to see George–' She put her hand to her mouth and looked worried. 'I don't think I was supposed to tell you that.'

'To see George? Mike's last secretary? The chap who wouldn't stay at Maidens?' Sam could see she was right.

'I suppose I'd better tell you, although I wasn't going to. Apparently, the police phoned Mike and asked him about George. He was amazed they knew George had worked for him. They didn't, of course, but 'it was George's print on the bolt.'

'Good heavens!'

'Exactly! And for some reason Mike wanted to see him.' Faye bit her lip. 'George did have a record from 'way back – he'd "borrowed" a bike when he was a kid. He was not known to be violent. Just the opposite, in fact, Pete said. That's all he had time to tell me. He was rushing off to try and see Frank Ross.'

'Mike mentioned Frank Ross. Who is he?'

'I don't know him. I think he had something to do with Jenny. Apparently he's just come out of prison. What is it, Sam?'

'I think Frank Ross must be the man in Jenny's Story. Mike changed all the names except Jenny's, but I reckon Ross is Jim.' Sam could see it didn't mean much to Faye.

'What a mess everything is, isn't it? How do you really feel now?'

'I was so scared, Faye. Thinking about it, I feel as though I've been scared for weeks and weeks. I just don't understand any of it. But, now, if it is George, then Mike was right when he said it could be someone mistakenly thinking they were getting at him by hurting me. After all, I don't know George from Adam!'

She looked at Faye's concerned face and forced herself to be cheerful.

Sam had already commented on her friend's blooming good looks and now demanded to be shown the nursery Faye said was nearly ready. They enjoyed a happy afternoon, until Sam said she should be going home.

'Didn't Mike tell you? He said you're to stay here.'

Sam stiffened, angry at not having been consulted.

'Sammy, be reasonable,' Faye urged. 'We'll all feel happier if we know you are safe. It's just until the police get that maniac. Pete says the man's obviously a nutter, and people like that are totally unpredictable.'

Sam nodded. 'You're right, it makes sense, love, and thank you. It's just that, on the train I decided I must get myself back to being me again. I seem to have lost some-thing – I always reckoned I was a strong person. But one of the reasons I split up from Derek was because he made most of the decisions, and I let him. It's as though I've been sagging and needing support.' She pulled a face, then her grin widened. 'And I sure can't stand mamby-pamby females. Why Kev and Robert would laugh their socks off if they knew the wimp their little sister had become.'

The two friends spent quite a long time arguing what was wimpish and what was commonsense as Sam unpacked her bags. Sam worried silently about Mike's meeting with George and when the phone rang she almost grabbed it before Faye could answer her own phone.

It was Pete and she went into her bedroom to give Faye a bit of privacy. Faye appeared happy enough, but as the evening wore on Sam watched her friend nervously twisting her wedding ring – round and round her finger.

'Are you trying to unscrew it?' Sam nodded pointedly at the ring. 'What's troubling you, Faye? Are you worried about Pete?'

'No. Well, yes, but...' She looked at Sam, then away, then back, then shook her head so distractedly that Sam went to sit beside her on the sofa and took hold of her hands.

'Now, just what did Pete say? You've been in a stew ever since he rang, though you told me everything was all right.' She was struck by a horrible thought. 'Is it Mike?'

Faye didn't answer and Sam wanted to shake her. 'Has something happened to Mike?'

'No – yes.'

CHAPTER NINE

Sick dread tightened inside her as Sam faced Faye. 'Tell me, Faye. What's wrong? What's happened to Mike?'

'Honestly, Sammy, he's all right.'

'Tell me.'

'He wasn't hurt, I promise, but his Range Rover was shot at when he went into the yard at the warehouse this morning.' She looked apologetic at Sam's horrified gasp. 'Pete didn't tell me before... This time the prints on the bolt were Frank Ross's!'

Sam broke the stunned silence.

'Frank Ross? I suppose that confirms Mike's theory, because I don't know this George, or Frank Ross. What a mess!' She raked her fingers through her hair. 'They'd have to think I'm pretty special to Mike. Huh, that's a laugh!'

They sat for a long time, not speaking.

'Sammy?' Faye hesitated. 'I – I don't like to pry–'

'Spit it out,' Sam encouraged. 'I won't answer if I don't want to.'

'I just wondered how you felt about Mike.'

'You know full well how I feel about him. I've been as good as telling you all afternoon, haven't I?'

Ignoring Sam's brusque manner, Faye hugged her in delight, but Sam smiling oddly, told her, 'Sorry, Faye. I might have fallen for him, but it doesn't follow that he feels the same.'

'Oh, but, surely…?' If it hadn't mattered so much, Sam would have laughed at her amazed disappointment. Faye's sunny nature saw happiness for everyone just around the corner. She had made the mistake good friends often did; the whole world must love the person they loved.

Sam had just fallen asleep when something wakened her. She was instantly alert – men's voices. She was out of bed and listening at the door before she could draw breath.

The relief when she heard Faye saying happily, 'I'd have stayed up if–'

Sam opened the door, remembering at the last minute to grab her dressing-gown, and rushed out to see Mike and Pete towering over Faye, also in her dressing-gown. Receiving the full power of double Manley, almost identical smiles, Sam beamed back, then enjoyed being taken into a pair of strong arms and held close.

Mike looked down at her and she was very nearly sure he returned her feelings. 'How are you?' The same soft words echoed each other's and they laughed and hugged again.

When they were all sitting down drinking coffee and brandy, the brothers related what had happened during the day to each of them.

'So poor old George is innocent and no-one knows where Frank is,' Pete summarised.

'But, just how did George's fingerprints

get on that bolt?' Sam wanted to know. 'It doesn't make sense to me – even if he is, as you say, innocent.'

'The crossbow was his originally. He'd taken it to the island without telling me,' Mike explained. 'And because he thought I might object, he hid it in the middle of the island, to use whenever he wanted. He likes to practise shooting at targets.'

'Yes,' Pete said, 'and he thought Mike had taken it away to stop him. Though neither of them mentioned it!'

'He sounds a bit wet, to me,' Sam said.

Mike nodded. 'I'm afraid he is.' He waited then said, 'Not so Frank Ross. And he's now been seen in Bristol. The Manor is the safest place, so we'll leave at first light.'

'No,' Sam said and ignored Mike's frown. 'I think you should take Faye up to Fort Knox, but I'll stay down here.'

'Absolutely not, Sam.'

'That's foolish!'

'You must come!'

After the three voices rang out together,

Sam said firmly, 'I'm going to my parents' house. In their little village any stranger would be noticed. I'll be all right there. If this nutter is after me, and it, unfortunately, looks like it, then I'm not putting Faye and the baby at risk.'

Sam would not be deterred and they made plans accordingly.

Faye was unknown to Frank Ross, and early next morning she drove out of the basement carpark in her own car with Pete lying down on the back seat. He was to stay out of sight until they could be sure no-one had followed them.

Sam took her time bathing and washing her hair, while Mike spent the morning on the phone. It was all right for him, he could carry on his normal business as though there was no Sword of Damocles hanging over them, damn him.

'I'll get off now, Mike,' she said shortly when he'd put the phone down after a particularly chummy conversation.

'It's gone quiet out there,' Mike said looking out of the window. He had spent the whole morning in that position and though nothing had been said, Sam knew he was watching out for Frank Ross.

'OK, I'll wait until there are more folk about. But Ross could be anywhere, miles away from here.'

'I wish you would reconsider, Sam. Or at least let me come with you. I don't like you being on your own.'

'It makes sense, Mike. Ross knows you.' She grinned. 'And you're so big he couldn't miss seeing you. Little me will not be so easy!'

It was a desperate attempt at lightness, but when Mike came towards her with his arms open she melted against him, wishing she could stay enfolded there for ever.

It was an hour later before there was the usual busy activity outside and Mike reluctantly said, 'Now is a good time to go, but don't forget, keep in touch. I'll ring you when I hear from Pete.'

He pulled her to him and lifted her face with a gentle hand, but Sam was aware of his restraint as he kissed her then opened the door.

The taxi rank outside the apartment block was busy with lots of people coming and going. Sam would have dearly liked to look up and wave; she knew Mike would be watching, but she must not draw attention to herself.

It went according to plan, but this time Sam felt no relief. Frank Ross, she had learned the night before, was definitely Jim in 'Jenny's Story.' Without doubt the man was violent and very probably unstable.

After she had taken her bags inside, Sam went to see her mother's next door neighbour. Sam told her she'd come home to avoid a boyfriend who wouldn't take no for an answer.

'Will you give me a ring if you see anybody about who shouldn't be? He can be rather unpleasant, I'm afraid, and I'd like to be able to phone the police if he gets too close.'

'And it might be as well if I keep coming to see to the post, just in case he asks questions in the village and knows your mum's away,' Mrs Jones volunteered, entering into the spirit. Her quick grasp of the situation and eager participation reminded Sam that Mrs Jones was an avid thriller reader.

On her own again Sam unpacked the food Faye had insisted she take, quite rightly saying there would be no food in her mother's house. She felt the siege mentality set in as she worked out how long the food would last, determined to make it last longer, in case – Idiot! Mrs Jones would be coming in each morning to see to the post and would get anything Sam needed.

She rang Mike as promised.

He answered on the second ring. 'Sam? Are you all right? I still think it would be better if I was with you.'

'Really, Mike. I'm fine. And I've got the next door neighbour keeping a look out for me.'

'Faye and Pete are settled in at The Manor,' he told her, but if he wished he were there, he didn't say. 'There's been no news yet from the police, but they'll soon track Frank down, now they know who they're looking for.'

'I hope so,' Sam said, not particularly reassured.

After a few seconds of silence Mike said, 'You know, Sam, I'd be much happier if you'd let me come and be with you. Being on your own and waiting for God knows what, is not a good idea.'

She overrode the feelings that gushed up just talking to him. Her determination to manage by herself came to the fore.

'That's sweet of you, Mike, but I am quite capable of looking after myself.' And she jolly well would, but only if she stopped taking support from all and sundry! 'I'll keep in touch.'

She went into the kitchen, opening cupboards and looking in the larder and planning a meal. Every nerve jumped as a dark shape passed the reeded window in the door.

She was relieved to hear the magpie's raucous squawk when a similar shape passed, and felt brave enough to look out of the kitchen window.

'One sorrow, two for joy ... thank goodness for that!' She laughed at her foolishness, then heard the phone ringing.

Sudden memory of her first phone call at The Manor made her listen before speaking. 'Sam? Sam is that you?'

'Yes, Mike. Is everything all right?'

'The Bristol police have just rung to say Frank Ross has been recognised in connection with a stolen car.'

'Are they sure it was him?'

'Yes, and he was heading north towards the motorway. You'll be all right now.' He paused, 'I'll ring you in the morning. Oh, Sam, I'll be glad when this is over. There's such a lot I want to say – better go now. Good-night, my dear, dear, Sam.'

Sam didn't know how long she sat there

beside the phone, but her daydreams were beautiful and she was loth to come back to the present.

She made up the bed in her old room. Then remembered she was supposed to be getting herself a meal.

Some time later, well-fed and only slightly anxious about Mike and Faye and Pete, she turned the television on for the late evening news. She wished she hadn't when there was no good news, but she stuck it out to see the weather. Huh, strong winds were to be expected. From the noise outside they had arrived, or it was the fox knocking Mrs Jones's dustbin lid off again. And broken a milk bottle by the sound of it.

Sam went into the kitchen just to check and reached across to the lightswitch. She didn't make it. Her arm was grabbed and twisted behind her back as an arm came round her neck and a hand covered her mouth.

CHAPTER TEN

'Shut up – don't make a sound,' a male voice ordered and Sam knew there was no point – no-one would hear anyway. 'Switch that light on, now.'

She flicked the switch.

Her head had moved a little when she reached for the light and she glimpsed the face of her captor. Her shock was total – it was the man on the train yesterday. Was he Frank Ross?

With her brain going like a steam engine she figured out what to do. She did not move, but waited for him to state his case.

'You won't make a sound, if you know what's good for you.' He took his hand away from her mouth and when she did nothing, he took his arm away, though still holding her arm behind her.

He pulled her arm further up her back, but he was disappointed if he thought she would cry out then he let her go. He grabbed the cook's knife from its woodblock and held it threateningly in front of him.

She could only stare at him. Then his eyes crinkled into a grin as he looked her over, as a farmer viewing a heifer at market.

'Very nice,' he drawled.

That did it! Fury ripped through her fear.

'Who are you? What do you want?' She fought to keep the tremors from her voice – sound calm, keep cool, but it had to be Frank Ross. Jenny's Jim. And she knew he was not averse to hitting women.

'Now that's no way to treat a guest, is it?'

'You're no guest, you're an intruder. Now get out before I call the police.' She kept her eyes off the knife – not knowing if she was being brave or foolhardy.

'Very good…' His lascivious eyes looked at her breasts and he licked his lips. 'Now you're what I call a woman. I like a bit of meat on my women.'

'I'm not your woman,' she snapped.

'You will be. Ask anyone–' He continued to smirk, and rocked on his heels. 'Frank Ross always gets what he wants. Of course, Mike Manley'll not like that, will he?' he gloated. 'Pity he ain't here to see, eh?'

He was mad. He didn't know her, nor she him. But Mike was right! This man had been scaring her half to death because he thought she was Mike's woman!

'Do you mean to say, you've come here because you think I am romantically connected with Mr Manley? Me?' She pointed to herself, then shook her head disbelievingly. 'I can't think who told you that rubbish. I know him, yes, but I only met Mike Manley recently – I'm a secretary – I've been temping for him.' She tried for wide eyed innocence and said, 'He's written a book you know, and I've just typed it for him.'

What had her self defence instructor said about psychopaths – keep them calm, go along with them as much as you can – they don't like being crossed.

Shivers slid down her back as his eyes narrowed and his mouth became a thin line. He was no longer smiling and she rushed on, 'I don't know for sure, but I think Mr Manley's girlfriend is the woman who is publishing his book.' She twisted her mouth disparagingly. 'That's the only way he's likely to get it published, if you ask me. It's rubbish.'

The formidable frown on Ross's face cleared slightly and Sam hoped she was convincing him.

'Have you eaten? Would you like me to cook something for you?'

'I like that,' Ross said. 'That's very thoughtful. Yes, I like that very much. I will have something to eat.' He waved her mother's razor sharp knife. 'Me stomach was beginning to think me throat 'ad been cut.'

He was grinning at his joke and Sam curved her lips to show she appreciated his humour.

Was this the right way to behave with a

psychopath? She tried hard to remember –
if she'd ever known. Praying she appeared
cool and composed, she got through some
time talking about what food there was in
the house. He seemed to enjoy choosing,
then changing his mind. At last he settled on
a cheese omelette and pickled onions and
fresh toast.

The heavy frying-pan was the ideal
weapon if she could only get close enough,
but whether he distrusted her, or whether
prison life had made him careful, he never
gave her the opportunity to bash him with
it.

Then he kept her busy with the toaster,
demanding his toast fresh just when he
wanted to eat it.

'You know,' he said expansively, 'You don't
never get good toast in the nick. You can
either mend your shoes with it or it's hard as
hard and cuts your mouth. But this is good.'

It must have been, she'd stopped counting
after the eighth piece.

Thank goodness there were jars of her

mother's own pickles in the larder, because Ross kept stabbing and eating the onions until he'd finished two jarsful. Then he leaned back on the kitchen chair and belched hugely. He grinned looking for Sam's approval – she gave it, grinning back and nodding her head. It was a mistake.

'What say you and me go upstairs, eh?' he suggested.

Alarm bells rang in her head – stay cool.

'Good idea,' she lied. 'But Mrs Jones, next door, said she'd pop round. We don't want her interfering, do we?' She pulled a face, adding, 'And it might be as well to let those onions go down a bit, heh?'

The thwarted, spoiled child's fury filled his face and she said quickly, 'But, tell me about you, Frank. I'd really like to know all about you.'

She tried to make it sound friendly, but not arousing, and added, 'When we met on the train, I had you down as a clever guy.'

She was casting about to remember dialogue from old gangster films. 'I bet you were framed, or you'd never have been in the nick, am I right?'

It was the magic button. Full of smiles, he said, 'Nearly right – I got meself put inside.'

The tension inside Sam dissolved a fraction. Frank was plainly delighted to have an appreciative audience to tell how brilliant he was.

'That stupid cow, Jenny, thought she'd given me the slip. But you gotta be up early to put one over on Frankie Ross.' He let that sink in. 'I followed her to Brum. I'm good at following – followed you...'

He remembered his story. 'Then I watched when Manley met her, then I had to pay a rotten taxi to follow them to his place. But the best was when I turned up a few days later – she thought she'd given me the slip, see – I just told her to get in the car – came good as gold, just like always – and I brought her back down to London.' He was very pleased with himself.

Sam nodded as expected, but could only be glad Mike was not here. Frank laughingly carried on. 'Silly cow jumped out at some lights and went down the Tube–'

'The Tube?'

'The Underground. You know – London Underground trains,' he explained.

'Go on. What happened then?'

'I followed her, of course.'

'What about the car?'

He looked surprised for a moment. 'What about it? I left it – it was only nicked.' Then he grinned sickeningly. 'The real laugh was, it was rush hour, wasn't it? She didn't see me behind her. I only gave her one little shove and I'd disappeared before the train hit her.'

Sam kept a lid on her reactions. And Frank was intent on telling all.

'I went to me local that night and a mate o' mine told me how he'd pulled a job down in Surrey – got some nice sparklers, and asked me if I wanted a ring for my Jen. Naturally, I said I'd look at it, 'cos she liked jewellery.'

Sam hated the crafty, clever-me look on

his face, while her own was aching with encouraging smiles.

'Well, as luck would have it, I'd just got it in my hand when the law collars me–'

'Never!' Sam gasped in false amazement.

He nodded approvingly. 'My mate'd disappeared, hadn't he? I hollered and shouted that they'd got the wrong bloke. Mind you, I didn't shout too loudly once I heard they was trying to pin Jenny's death on me – said she'd been murdered–'

'They never…' Sam gasped yet again. She could see he didn't think his one little push that sent Jenny under the train should count as murder.

Suddenly, he stabbed the knife into the wooden table, took it out and stabbed again and again. His eyes were vacant.

'How about a cup of tea, or better – a whisky?' Sam offered, trying to distract him.

'Yeh, good idea. I'm partial to a whisky and I'll have a cup o' tea.'

Sam went through into the dining-room, exercising the muscles in her face while he couldn't see. She knew she was taking a chance with the whisky, but if he would only drink the lot, then perhaps she would be safe.

She fetched a full bottle of her father's whisky and a glass and, smiling again, she poured him a large measure.

'Ta,' he said, surprising her.

Not hurrying, she filled the kettle and switched it on. 'Is that OK?' she asked when he'd taken a drink.

'Yeh. It's been a long time since I had whisky. I'm a pints guy really.'

She used all her ingenuity to lead him on and keep him talking through to the small hours. She made tea every hour and watched the whisky disappear down the bottle while she learned all about his 'rotten' treatment inside.

Once she thought he had fallen asleep, and moved nearer to the knife, but he stirred and carried on talking.

She heard how he'd gone to Mike's works and chatted up the young receptionist to find out where Mike was. As Frank told her about going to the island he seemed to have forgotten it was she who had been his target. He got all strung up again as he repeated it was Mike Manley's fault that he'd lost his Jenny and he, Frank was going to take out Manley's woman.

'Can I help?' Sam's eager question brought a look of approval.

'Sure, why not. We'll make a good team.'

Then the sound of birds calling told them morning was about to break and she knew she must get Frank Ross away from the house. Perhaps the whisky had not been a good idea, as he carved more savagely at her mother's kitchen table, then was maudlin in turns.

'Frank,' she said huskily. 'What say you and me split before it gets light? Have you got a car?'

He looked eager, then furious. Sam dare not encourage him further, but waited, desperately afraid she had said the wrong thing.

'You know,' he said keenly, 'I reckon we

should get out of here before it's light.'

'That's a brilliant idea, Frank,' Sam said, ready to play any game that would get them out of the house.

'Yeah, I'll soon get us a car. They ain't made the car that can stop Frankie Ross. Fifteen seconds top whack – in and away.'

Sam nearly jumped a mile when the phone rang in the hall. 'I'd better answer it, they know I'm here.' Thank goodness he didn't want to know who 'they' were. Frank's face showed a jumble of emotions and he was almost hopping up and down.

'Yeah, OK,' he said quickly.

'Mr Manley's secretary, can I help you? Yes, but–' she listened, grimacing and shrugging her shoulders for Frank's benefit. 'Sorry, I can't give you any more inform-ation. I'm just going for a drive with my friend. Goodbye.' She put the phone down and said, 'Let's get out of here, quick, before some other fool rings.'

Sam grabbed her jacket and followed Frank through the kitchen and out of the back door, not bothering to lock it. They dashed down the path at the front of the house, then Frank stood surveying the collection of cars parked on the road. But before he'd chosen there was the sound of tyres cornering too fast and two police-cars came screaming to a stop twenty feet away.

CHAPTER ELEVEN

Frank caught hold of her arm and she knew he was taking no chances. Sam's heart stopped when she saw Mike get out of his Range Rover behind the police cars.

Three young policemen were coming towards them.

'Let her go, Ross. You can't get away.'

'Stay where you are, or she gets it.' And Sam's arm was twisted behind her again, but this time the razor-sharp knife was put against her neck.

'Don't be stupid, Frank,' Mike said. 'You know it's me you want.' He walked forward to stand in front of the policemen. Sam felt a prick on her neck and saw from Mike's reaction that there was blood. He took another step forward.

'Stop!' Frank screamed, and they all heard

the dangerously-near-the-edge note in his voice.

'OK, OK, but what is it you want, Frank?' Mike placated.

'That's better. Now turn your car around and leave the engine running.' He turned to the police, waving the knife threateningly, 'You lot get back in the cars.' For the first time Sam noticed two men in ordinary suits near a high performance black car. They were obviously higher-ranking police officers and signalled for Frank to be obeyed.

'Now we're going,' Frank whispered in Sam's ear and led her to where Mike had turned his Range Rover.

'Shall I drive, Frank?'

'You what? A dame drive Frankie Ross? I should cocoa!'

He pushed Sam forward, 'Get out,' he shouted at Mike before Sam opened the door. As she climbed up into the high vehicle, Frank caught Mike off balance and dragged him out by his jacket lapel, stabbing at him as he fell and yelling, 'It's all your fault, if my Jenny hadn't run off wi' you – she'd be 'ere now.'

Before Sam could get over the centre console to help Mike, Frank was in and driving as though all the hounds in hell were on his tail.

The four-wheel drive Range Rover took the soggy village green effortlessly. Then Frank looked back and laughed out loud to see the police cars stuck in the mud.

As they drove towards Bristol, Frank calmed a little and Sam swallowed a mixture of relief and exasperation. His driving would not draw attention to them, despite all the whisky he'd drunk, and Sam wracked her brains to think of a way out. She could always hope for a red light and do as Jenny had done.

The traffic was much heavier when they reached the city. Frank's patience gave out. Banging on the hooter, then holding it down whenever there was a slight hold up, seemed to give him more energy to shout and swear at the other drivers. Then he objected to the others stopping for red lights and drove on the other side of the road, round bollards and cut other drivers up so he could keep going.

They heard a police car behind them, then another did a U-turn in the road to chase after them. Laughing and swearing at the police spurred Frank to even faster speed and wilder driving. Sam had automatically put on her seat belt, thank goodness, and now clung to it as they swerved round corners like something from the old Keystone Cops films. But it was not funny.

Sam no longer recognised this area of Bristol and she saw they were in an industrial estate. The huge lorries were like skittles to bounce off and Frank was enjoying the game. He swore violently and Sam could see no way out – it was a dead end. There was only an empty-looking, derelict factory. He drove through the vandalised factory doors and jumped out, shouting for Sam to hurry up.

She was still searching for the handle to

lock herself in, when he came round and yanked her out. He dragged her to her feet and pulled her along with him.

'I couldn't find the handle,' she said breathlessly, gaining her balance.

Sam heard the screech of brakes and tyres outside. 'Hurry up,' she told him, pretending to be eager to go with him. He was still holding her wrist tightly, and she used that to stretch his arm, then put all her weight behind her other fist to whack his elbow joint the wrong way. Ignoring his scream of pain, she managed to trip him at the same time. Then she ran. She kept on going, passing several policemen as she went through the wrecked door.

Sam looked at the faces of the men outside, but Mike was not there.

'Are you all right?'

Sam shook off the caring hand of the policewoman and breathlessly demanded, 'Where's Mike? Why isn't he here? Is he all right? I was sure he would be here.'

'Come and sit in the car for a minute. Give

yourself a chance to get your breath.'

'I don't want to get my breath! I want to know what happened to Mike Manley. Tell me,' she said through gritted teeth as her self control stretched towards breaking point. 'Oh, dear God, he's not...?'

Praying as never before, Sam heard the policewoman report, 'Mr Manley has been taken to hospital. I'm not sure of the extent of his injuries.'

'Take me to the hospital – now!' About to get in the police car, she noticed one of the grey-suited men had heard her demand.

'We'll see you get there as soon as possible. I don't think Mr Manley's injuries are life threatening, but he'll be pleased to see you in one piece, Sam.' He shut the door when she was seated and she heard him summon the driver.

Mike looked a bit pale sitting up in bed, his chest and one arm covered in dressings, but his eyes lit with joy when he saw her.

Not sure if she was glad that the other

beds in the small ward were empty, Sam was suddenly shy, doubtful again.

'How do you feel, Mike?'

'All the better for seeing you.' He held his injured arm to her and she grasped his hand, holding it to her face, then kissing it. 'I don't want to live through anything like this morning again – as soon as you said, "Mr Manley's secretary," I knew Ross was there. And I was phoning you to warn you that Ross might be about – they'd found the car that he stole down in Bath. He obviously doubled back after we thought he was going north.'

He pulled her close, kissing her eyes, nose, lips and she wanted to cry she was so happy. 'Oh, Sam, if anything had happened to you–'

'It didn't, and you can stop blaming yourself, Mike Manley. And feeling guilty about Jenny. I have news for you...'

Very quietly, but as quickly as she could she repeated all that Frank Ross had told her the night before. Holding his hand and loving him so much, she could not stop the love shining in her eyes.

Two people in love was what Pete saw a little while later when he came to visit.

'Don't know what made me come back down this morning, but I took Faye to her mother's and high-tailed it here – probably this twin thing,' he said, 'and friends in the police.'

Then his grin widened, he could see his brother was catching up fast in the family stakes. He'd hoped Sam was the future wife Mike had hinted at and Faye would be more than pleased.

When he had been brought up to date on Frank Ross's revelations, he said, 'Well, it seems like he got what he deserved.'

'What do you mean?' Sam and Mike said together, puzzled.

'Gosh, hasn't anybody told you? After you made your escape, Sam, Frank went up to the top of that building and tried to jump across to another one. He didn't make it. Killed outright.'

Deserved or not, Sam felt an enormous sense of relief. Mike was safe and they would not have to worry and wonder where Frank Ross was anymore. Mike's grip had tightened and she knew he felt the same.

'Sister said they'll let you go home if you have someone to look after you. Want me to stay and look after you?' Pete asked. 'No, I didn't think you would,' he said with a grin as he watched Sam's blushing smile answer Mike's uncertainty. 'Shall I wait to take you back to the flat?'

'Thanks, Pete,' his brother said, 'but we'll get a taxi.'

'Well, I've a wife who needs me, so I'll be off.' He gripped his brother's good hand and gently play-punched his shoulder. 'Take care, Big Bruv. And you, Sam.' He kissed her then left.

The Sister came in when Mike was dressed and smiled as she handed Sam a card. 'You will make sure he comes for the rest of his tetanus shots, won't you? These men find it convenient to forget, sometimes.' She left them and Sam pulled a face at the invalid.

'Oh, so your shots weren't up to date? Well, well, well! I must remember to check before I agree to go to a lonely island in the middle of winter – if my boss should ask me, of course.'

She saw from Mike's sheepish grin that he remembered.

'Does that mean you would come again if I asked you, Sam?'

'Oh, yes – I'd love to see it in the spring,' she teased. 'And summer and autumn...' Her voice was deep and low as she told him, 'I'll go any time – anywhere, so long as you are there.'

'Oh, my dear love,' he said huskily, gathering her in his arms. Their kiss stirred both hearts to undreamed of happiness and a newly-arrived patient coughed twice before they knew they were not alone.

All three shared a good-humoured grin, before Mike and Sam hurried out to find a taxi.

'Well, Mrs Manley, how does it feel being married to a famous author?'

It was more than a year later and they were attending a special re-print party for 'Jenny's Story.'

'It will feel brilliant, Mr Manley, when these twins of yours stop kicking their mother. I'm sure they'll be born with football boots on.'

She gave him a stern stare, then burst out laughing. She couldn't stay cross, even pretend cross, for two minutes with her darling husband.

Barbara, Mike's plump, motherly editor thought she had never seen a happier young couple.

'You know,' she said, turning back to the bookseller, 'it might seem a bit harsh, but the reading public like the ending because they say Jim deserved to die. Just desserts and all that...'

The publishers hope that this book has given you enjoyable reading. Large Print Books are especially designed to be as easy to see and hold as possible. If you wish a complete list of our books please ask at your local library or write directly to:

Dales Large Print Books
Magna House, Long Preston,
Skipton, North Yorkshire.
BD23 4ND

This Large Print Book, for people
who cannot read normal print,
is published under the auspices of
THE ULVERSCROFT FOUNDATION

... we hope you have enjoyed this book.
Please think for a moment about those
who have worse eyesight than you ...
and are unable to even read or enjoy
Large Print without great difficulty.

You can help them by sending a
donation, large or small, to:

**The Ulverscroft Foundation,
1, The Green, Bradgate Road,
Anstey, Leicestershire, LE7 7FU,
England.**
or request a copy of our brochure for
more details.

The Foundation will use all donations
to assist those people who are visually
impaired and need special attention
with medical research, diagnosis
and treatment.

Thank you very much for your help.